PENGUIN BOOKS

DEAREST DOROTHY, ARE WE THERE YET?

Charlene Ann Baumbich is a popular speaker, journalist, and author. Her stories, essays, and columns have appeared in numerous magazines and newspapers, including the *Chicago Tribune,* the *Chicago Sun-Times,* and *Today's Christian Woman.* She is also the author of the second novel in the Partonville series, *Dearest Dorothy, Slow Down, You're Wearing Us Out!,* and six books of nonfiction. She lives in Glen Ellyn, Illinois. Learn more about Charlene at www.welcometopartonville.com.

ALSO IN THIS SERIES

Dearest Dorothy, Slow Down, You're Wearing Us Out!

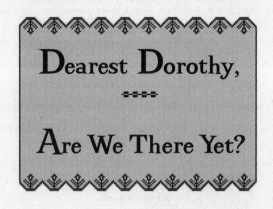

Dearest Dorothy,

Are We There Yet?

Charlene Ann Baumbich

PENGUIN BOOKS

PENGUIN BOOKS

Published by the Penguin Group

Penguin Group (USA) Inc., 375 Hudson Street, New York, New York 10014, U.S.A.
Penguin Group (Canada), 90 Eglinton Avenue East, Suite 700, Toronto,
Ontario, Canada M4P 2Y3 (a division of Pearson Penguin Canada Inc.)
Penguin Books Ltd, 80 Strand, London WC2R 0RL, England
Penguin Ireland, 25 St Stephen's Green, Dublin 2, Ireland (a division of Penguin Books Ltd)
Penguin Group (Australia), 250 Camberwell Road, Camberwell,
Victoria 3124, Australia (a division of Pearson Australia Group Pty Ltd)
Penguin Books India Pvt Ltd, 11 Community Centre, Panchsheel Park, New Delhi – 110 017, India
Penguin Group (NZ), cnr Airborne and Rosedale Roads,
Albany, Auckland 1310, New Zealand (a division of Pearson New Zealand Ltd)
Penguin Books (South Africa) (Pty) Ltd, 24 Sturdee Avenue,
Rosebank, Johannesburg 2196, South Africa

Penguin Books Ltd, Registered Offices: 80 Strand, London WC2R 0RL, England

First published in the United States of America by Guideposts Books 2002
Published in Penguin Books 2004

7 9 10 8

PUBLISHER'S NOTE

This is a work of fiction. Names, characters, places, and incidents either are the product of the author's imagination or are used fictitiously, and any resemblance to actual persons, living or dead, business establishments, events, or locales is entirely coincidental.

LIBRARY OF CONGRESS CATALOGING-IN-PUBLICATION DATA
Baumbich, Charlene Ann, 1945–
[Are we there yet?]
Dearest Dorothy, are we there yet?/ Charlene Ann Baumbich.
p. cm.
ISBN 0-14-200379-4
1. Aged women–Fiction.   2. Illinois–Fiction   I. Title.
PS3602.A963A88 2004
813'.54–dc21   2003049860

Printed in the United States of America

Set in Berthold Garamond
Designed by Sabrina Bowers

Dedicated to the real *Oldster Characters
in my life who inspired creativity;
taught sensitivity; modeled kindness,
acceptance and wahoo fun;
were unabashedly their own True Selves;
and cheered me on—all the way from heaven.
Especially my Dearest Dorothy.*

Acknowledgments

How do I begin to thank everyone who helped wing these books to life? I mean, the cast of characters (real ones) is huge! Although I have already written my dedication page to the Masters of My Inspiration, there are OH! so many more friends, family and just plain good folks who helped knit these books together. Their range of contributions is nothing short of astounding: inspiration ("I know you can, I know you can"); education (teaching me details about stuff I know nothing about so that my fiction doesn't get too many "I don't think so!" responses from you astute readers); cheerleading ("Great chapter!"); shrink duty ("Yes, sometimes 'reality' is slippery, Charlene"); hysteria stopping ("Snap out of it!"); listening to me whine (yes, I do my fair share). And a WAHOO! thanks for friends who never gave up on me, even when I was impossible; who provided laughs when I needed them, breaks when I needed them, tolerance when I needed it, mercy when I needed it and a kick in the butt when I needed it.

Without Terri Castillo, there would be no *Dearest Dorothy* books. Her verbalized question became the materialized project. She asked; I knew; it was. (Okay, there were years of hard work and creative flying in the midst of this, but the short and True Birthing Miracle version is this: She asked; I knew; it was.) As I type, I pray blessings upon her journey. She has gently launched me with full spiritual sails into the delicious waters of Story.

Regina Hersey, my editor, was a constant bellows to the all of my all (and she'll probably tell me "'the all of my all' doesn't make sense," but I'm writing these acknowledgments and she'll just have to live with it—HA!). Again, without Regina, no *Dearest Dorothy* books. Simple as that. From the very first e-mail forwarded to me after she read my first draft, to the very last conversation I've had with her (which was probably yesterday, since she's become my True Friend), she has been nothing short of a pure-gold gift. I have no doubt that our synergy was God designed, and 'twas the genius of Terri Castillo who matched us up. Even though I sometimes quake at Regina's ability to be a self-ordained Grammar Nazi who always has "just a few little things" for me to address in my manuscripts, she is, without exception, grace upon grace in my life.

Oftentimes we need a mentor who has honorably journeyed down the road before us. Novelist Terri Blackstock graciously gave me ninety minutes of her time during one frantic, out-of-the-blue phone call. It was ninety minutes' worth of genuine, literal, literary and Big Picture guidance. My journey became instantly lighter and wiser.

Between *Are We There Yet?* and *Slow Down, You're Wearing Us Out!* the following are people who fell into that "education" category I mentioned before, going above and beyond the call of duty to help guide a stranger through the back roads of things like commercial real estate development, long-haul moving, heart conditions, auto repair, demolition derby and a host of other details: Steve Gibson, Larry Alexander, Thomas Wood, Harold Benware, Dave Thompson, Bruce Bradley, Mary S., Donna Manley, Robin

Webb, Joanne Boppart and Gregory Baumbich, who, against his Chevy heart but for the love of family, talked to me about a Ford product. My apologies to anyone I left out before this rolled to press. Your exclusion implies no less importance but speaks to my fuzzy, midlife brain cells.

The folks at Guideposts Books and Inspirational Media Division, especially Elizabeth Kramer Gold and her snappy sense of humor, were definitely guideposts. I thank them for their courage and their ministry.

The first time I met Carolyn Carlson, both my professional and personal life brightened. Her enthusiasm for the first two books in the Partonville series, and her sensitivities to what *really* matters in *all* of life—which is the same message in the novels—made for a rousing combination. When it became official that Penguin Books would be bringing the books into book stores, a shout of joy erupted from my soul (once I stopped freaking out), which has yet to stop twirling with delight.

And to my husband, George, I give my utmost thanks for standing watch at the door to Our World. He has countless times stood there alone, staring down the road (or up the stairs to my office, or into my eyes), waiting for me to return from Partonville. I love you, my Honey Bunny.

Introduction

To be seventy years young is sometimes far more cheerful and hopeful than to be forty years old.
—Oliver Wendell Holmes

And now, welcome to Partonville, a circle-the-square town in the northern part of southern Illinois, where oldsters are young, trees have names and cars don't fly.

Dearest Dorothy,

✖✖✖✖

Are We There Yet?

1

A powerful CRACK! broke the pre-dawn hush as a bolt of lightning seared into the field, briefly illuminating the clapboard farmhouse. Dorothy Jean Wetstra's eyes flew open and her body lurched. Up until that moment, she'd been deep in sleep, curled up on her side, nesting in a warm sea of ancient quilts.

She rolled to her back and lay there, stiff as a board, staring unblinking at the ceiling. Once her heart finally stopped hammering, fits of tossing and turning kept her awake long after the booming and rumbling had passed. In the aftermath of silence, the rain-drenched and ripened farmland beckoned her into its respite. She'd once read that nature was a glove on the hand of God, and she knew she'd read Truth. She finally gave up on sleep and decided to take her charged energies for a swift walk, hoping not only to extinguish their dominion over her tired body, but also to rest in the quiet hands of the Creator.

Dorothy swung her legs over the side of the tall bed and slowly straightened her stately five-foot-ten-inch frame, waiting for the night's body kinks to work themselves out. Since she always slept with at least one bedroom window open, the cool, damp April air spurred her into action to pull on her clothes. Pink—her trademark color—sweat suit, white socks and Keds in place, she whisked into the bathroom, put in her partial plate, then looked in the mirror at her sleepy brown eyes and wispy white locks. "Hair, you're on your own until I return."

Sheba, her eight-year-old constant companion—dubbed "Queen of the Mutt Dogs" the day Dorothy discovered the brown-and-black pup in the ditch—raised her head from the end of Dorothy's bed and stared at her. "You're either comin' or not, but I'm going to the creek," Dorothy said, hands on her hips. Sheba stood, stretched back on her haunches, gave a widemouthed yawn and leapt to the floor, right on Dorothy's heels. Sheba wasn't one to be left behind. She needed to spring into action if she wanted to keep up with her energetic master—although some in Partonville might question who mastered whom.

The journey down Dorothy's steep staircase, into the living room, through the kitchen, out the back door, past the giant white barn, then along the cornfields down to the creek was invigorating. Although she could have negotiated the familiar path with her eyes closed, she relished each step. The last moody shades of pink sunrise had finished their dance by the time she stood creekside in the silence.

Like the comforting lullaby of a mother, the coo of a mourning dove spoke straight to her heart. For a moment, a single sound of a moment, she forgot about her predicament, and all that existed was the fresh wind of spring bursting into her worried, wintered soul. In that bright instant, the beauty of the meandering creek and the farmland beneath her feet held her safe.

Just as quickly, the dove fell silent and the rapid beating of Dorothy's anxious heart once again rocked her security. What would, what *could* her life be like were she to sell this farm, which had embraced and nurtured all eighty-seven years of her life?

Dorothy stepped down the slight embankment to the edge of the water and studied its brisk current. Although mud squished up the sides of the rubber trim on her tennis shoes, she never worried about mess or cockleburs when she was roaming the land. The earthy aroma rendered by her very steps was as pleasing as any highfalutin perfume she'd whiffed. Black Illinois dirt was something to celebrate and receive with all your senses. "God's creatures don't melt when it rains or shrivel when they're dirty," she'd often said, and she lived every word.

Dorothy recalled days from her youth when decisions had been made by the simplest of means: a "lefty-or-righty, righty-or-wrongy twig." She grinned at the absurdity of the method, but also at the fun of the process. Of course, what decision did any ten-year-old have to make that really mattered to the grand scheme of life? If Dorothy sold her land to a developer, the ramifications would have much more impact than the youthful consequences of whether or not to dive in the swimmin' hole on a chilly day, or whether or not to tell May Belle she had a crush on somebody. Now, were she to sell her farm, not only would her life change, but so would the entire future of Partonville.

And yet, the true country girl who dwelled within couldn't resist; she began hunting for the perfect "lefty-or-righty, righty-or-wrongy twig," humming the song she and her best friend, May Belle, had composed more than seven decades ago.

Lefty or righty, righty or wrongy,
tell me true while we sing this songy.

Wish we may, wish we might,
have you reveal if we're wrong or right.

No sooner had Dorothy finished the tune than her eyes landed on the perfect twig. She scooped it up and turned to show it to Sheba, who had wandered off somewhere, probably hot on the trail of some poor critter. Holding it firmly, she closed her eyes, created her righty-wrongy choices—which changed from incident to incident—and spoke her decision aloud.

"Left of the rock is wrongy and I don't sell, right of the rock is righty and I accept the offer with Craig & Craig Developers." She stepped back into the squishy mud, leaned over and, with great ceremonial dignity, tossed the stick into the middle of the rushing waters.

Off it sailed toward the Big Rock in the middle of the creek just before the bend, where all righty-wrongy determinations were made. Holding her breath, she squinted to keep the twig in sight, knowing how easily it could be lost in the current. Within a few seconds, the righty-wrongy twig raced into the middle of the rock where it . . . LODGED! It was going neither right nor left around the rock. Immediately after the twig hit the rock, a three-foot-long, three-inch-thick branch pinned the twig to the back of the boulder and a barrage of other twigs and branches instantly joined the dam. It looked like an entire beaver town had broken apart upstream and swallowed her twig alive. Dorothy realized she was still holding her breath, and she gushed a whooshing exhalation, staring, staring. . . .

The pile began to shift and rock and finally broke itself apart, splitting down the middle, some going left and some going right, her twig lost in the shuffle.

"Lord," she said aloud, "You and I know it was just a silly girlhood game anyway. But I'm needing an answer! I'm plumb worn out from sleepless nights, praying and thinking about this decision, remembering all the years of my life on this land—as a girl, a wife . . . a mother myself.

"And yet, I'm eighty-seven, and my children are growed up and gone. Gone. That's the reality. And we both know my old ticker isn't what it used to be and nothing stays the same and change is sneaking up on us anyway and I have this hunch it's just time to move on while I still have my senses and can make the choice myself and . . ." Her voice trailed off as she ran out of breath releasing the exploding thoughts. She walked a few steps, kicking aside twigs and clumps of last year's damp leaves, praying the way it came naturally, with her eyes wide open, just chatting away with Jesus.

"Now You tell me in Your Word that You know every hair on my now mostly pink-scalped head. You know my comings and my goings and You knit me in my mother's womb. Is it too much to ask, in the middle of all Your counting and knitting, that You give me one little answer?" She looked up at the bright morning sky, hands on her hips—like Job, challenging the One who loved her.

"Okay. I'm done talking now and ready to listen. I promise. Amen." Dorothy stood still as a post, watching the waters race to wherever they were going next. The mourning dove cooed, and for a moment, another single sound of a joy-filled moment, she knew she had an answer, even though she wasn't sure what it was.

Dorothy made her way back to the house and fixed herself a cup of tea and a slice of toast slathered with butter and sprinkled with sugar, her personal version of "cooking" dessert for breakfast. She washed her face, fixed her hair and fed Sheba, then finally felt mentally strong enough to try once again to plow her way through the Craig & Craig offer. She sat down at the massive mahogany desk that had served for more than a century as a cornerstone in the dining room. It was once her father's father's; she felt connected to heritage whenever she stroked her hand against the well-cared-for wood. Slowly she opened the file, glanced at the offer's expiration date, May 3—she'd had the offer for nearly a month—and then at her calendar, April 22.

"Sheba!" she yelped. Sheba jumped up off the floor near the radiator and began barking. "It's May Belle's birthday today! I've been so selfish, worrying about me, that I've forgotten my best friend's birthday!" She closed the file, tossed it toward the back of the desk and briskly walked to her kitchen phone, fingers flying over the keypad. After listening to Dorothy sing "Happy Birthday" clear through twice, May Belle happily accepted her friend's offer to buy her a birthday lunch at Harry's.

Lester K. Biggs, "Sole Proprietor of Harry's Grill," as it said on his business cards, grumbled a bit about Dorothy's last-minute fussing around, just when the early lunch crowd was at its height. She'd arrived in a flurry, stormed into the grill, tossed her giant handbag on a chair at the table in the front window—right under the MAXIMUM SEATING 25. NO CREDIT CARDS & NO CHECKS! sign—and retrieved an old-fashioned, pointy birthday hat from her pink nylon backpack. Whisking up to the U-shaped counter, she helped herself to the last of the sweet rolls left in the display near the cash register. She also helped herself to a plate from behind the counter, which was what really got Lester to bristling, since this was definitely his territory. Because it was Dorothy, he let it slide, but not without huffing around a bit to let her know she'd violated the rules of the establishment.

Dorothy took the sweet roll to the table, rummaged through her backpack and produced a box of partially burned birthday candles, which without counting she stuck in the sweet roll, this way and that. *Eighty-six candles would probably burn the place down anyway!* she thought. She alerted everyone at the counter that as soon as May Belle entered, they were to watch for Dorothy's cue to sing "Happy Birthday." Even if they didn't feel like singing, like Lester, they'd make an exception for Dorothy, since she was, well, Dorothy and they all loved and respected this spunky woman who had, over the decades, become a kind of town matriarch.

Seating herself facing the door, she waited for May Belle to arrive. May Belle walked in just a few moments later, accompanied by her son, Earl, another of Dorothy's favorite people in the whole wide world. May Belle and Homer had, much to their surprise, conceived their only child late in life. Never a day passed when Earl wasn't viewed and loved by them as nothing short of a "bright miracle." Although Earl was mentally challenged, he was lovingly described, enjoyed and accepted by folks in Partonville as "slow and particular. That's just the way Earl is."

Dorothy leapt to her feet and welcomed her friend with a hug. As soon as she'd secured the rubber strapping to the birthday hat around May Belle's plump chin, she turned to the folks at the counter. They had all swiveled toward her. Eyebrows up, head tilted back, Dorothy lifted her hand high over her head, held it poised for an attention-commanding moment—she had been a bandleader all her working life— hummed a note suitable to her aged tenor voice, then sliced her hand down through the air with the first of the three-beat motions, leading the entire group at Harry's Grill in singing "Happy Birthday."

May Belle broke out in laughter when Dorothy made them hold the last note so long she thought they might all tumble off their stools, gasping for breath. Everyone clapped, then returned to eating as the two women seated themselves at the table. Earl, who had already eaten lunch at home, had disappeared when all the uncomfortable attention had turned their way. Dorothy and May Belle understood, knowing he'd headed home, one block off the square, where things were normal.

After ordering their food—hamburgers and fries, their favorite since grammar school—May Belle said, "Dorothy, you really look tired, and it's not the first time I've noticed that lately. Are you feeling okay, dear?"

Dorothy silently studied her best friend for a moment, so needing to talk to *someone* about her tormenting decision. But she knew May Belle couldn't be impartial. For years May Belle had expressed how it worried her that Dorothy was so far out in the country, all alone. "At our age," she used to begin, "things can happen, Dorothy, and no one would even know it! Maybe it's time for you to *unburden* yourself from that old farm and move into town." But Dorothy always resisted, unable to put the words *farm* and *burden* in the same sentence. No, May Belle was too devoted to her friend to worry about the community as a whole. And besides, Dorothy knew May Belle had enough on her mind, fretting and praying about what might one day happen to Earl when the Lord took *her* home.

"Do you mean to tell me you slept right through that storm this morning?" Dorothy said, skirting the issue.

"Storm?"

"Oh, May Belle! You could sleep through an earthquake, I imagine." Dorothy was about to ask her if she remembered the "lefty-or-righty, righty-or-wrongy twig" when May Belle thankfully changed the subject.

"Say, did you hear about Tess Walker? Poor thing. I haven't actually seen her for years. I feel terrible she died so alone."

"Yes. I heard. Cora Davis phoned me. I guess she saw the ambulance out in front of Tess's house when they wheeled her body away. Honestly, that woman just seems to have a nose for news. Hasn't changed a lick since she was secretly voted third grade's biggest tattletale!" May Belle and Dorothy grinned, aware they were sitting in Cora's usual seat, right in the window from which at least half of the town square could be spied upon.

Dorothy said, "I imagine Tess's niece in Chicago will be the one who has to come and deal with arrangements and her estate, such as it is. I don't believe Tess had another living relative."

"You'd know better than me. You and Tess used to visit on occasion, the way I remember it. Of course, her baby sister always had to tag along. I just never got to know either of them much more than to say a howdy do."

After hesitating a moment, Dorothy said quietly, "Yes, I guess I got to know those sisters about as well as anyone. They were so close . . ." Her voice trailed off and she swirled her coffee mug, watching the last drops coat the bottom. Somberly, she continued: "I tell you, when her sister, Clarice, moved to Chicago, it about broke Tess's heart in two. Set her into an unlifting depression. And Tess wasn't much of a traveler anyway. Always did like to be home, sleeping in her own bed."

"I can relate to that," May Belle said. "Some of us," and she nodded her head at Dorothy, "just tend to have a bit more gypsy in our souls than others." Although Dorothy loved her farm, she would travel just about anywhere via any means at the drop of a hat, chanting "Road Trip, Road Trip" to the tune of a doorbell and asking within minutes of their departure, "Are we there yet?"

When they'd polished off their last French fry, Dorothy held her mug in the air to catch Lester's attention. She needed one final steaming cup to go with dessert. They lingered a spell, May Belle letting Dorothy eat most of the sweet roll, knowing her penchant for sugary anything.

"Well," Dorothy said, wiping her mouth with her paper napkin, "I better get home to Sheba, though she's probably still sleeping. She plumb exhausted herself during our early morning jaunt to the creek. I had to holler three times before she finally appeared, dripping wet and full of mud, grinning from ear to ear. It must have been quite the chase. I pity the animal!

"I'll see you tomorrow at the Hookers meeting. I hope you're spending the day baking!" Dorothy said as she gathered her handbag and backpack and headed for the door.

2

Dust flew up off the gravel road while rocks clatter-banged their own frenzied rhythm on the exhaust. The Tank, as Dorothy loved to call her rusty-and-white 1976 Lincoln Continental, fishtailed coming out of the thirty-degree bend in the road, the last curve before the half-mile straightaway into town. At least that's the way Dorothy viewed it.

"Full throttle," she hollered to Sheba as the battle-worn Tank finally shimmied and skidded her way due west. Dorothy reveled in the freedom to travel just the way she liked: fast. Her short, thinning snow-white hair rippled in the breeze of the open windows like a field of dried dandelions.

Sheba steadied herself against the swaying backseat, then resumed her position in the window once The Tank flattened out. Tongue sailing, ears flapping parallel with her tongue, twelve-pound Sheba made the perfect copilot. If Lincoln Continentals could fly, undoubtedly she and Dorothy would be airborne by now, such was the height of their exhilaration. But alas, cars didn't fly, not even over the back roads of Partonville.

"Hang on, Sheba! I'm gonna see if we can't make sixty!" As if she understood English (and most in Partonville thought she did), Sheba spread her hind legs a bit wider.

The Tank topped out at sixty-two before Dorothy started backin' her down to make the stop sign for the T intersection at the hard road.

Dorothy was on her way to the monthly meeting of the Happy Hookers Club, and she sure didn't want to miss a minute of this one. Maggie Malone, seventy-two-year-old Hooker member and owner-operator of La Feminique Hair Salon & Day Spa, was back from her annual trek to Chicago for a regional hairdressers' convention, and the Happy Hookers couldn't wait to see what she looked like. Every year's convention presented Maggie with an opportunity for an exciting, outrageous adventure. Though a lifetime resident of Partonville, business owner, wife, mother of nine, grandmother of eight and great-grandmother of three (Maggie was a woman who relished and lived extremes), she truly loved being away where she could let the "Real Maggie" out, as she told her clients. Why, one year she'd returned with mahogany-colored hair!

Dorothy zoomed up in front of May Belle's at the stroke of 7:00 P.M. Nearly simultaneously, she turned off the engine, kicked open the door and began unfolding herself upright. As usual, she was dressed in pink from her turtleneck to the curlicue laces in her white gym shoes. Once erect, she slung her giant black vinyl handbag over her shoulder and then slammed the door. Realizing it didn't close just right, with all that was within her she slammed it again and hollered to the universe, "Arthur Landers! Some mechanic you are! Next time FIX that door!" Then with one swift motion, Dorothy, eyes glistening with mischief, turned toward the back window, steadied herself and held out her arms. Sheba catapulted through the open window, right into them.

"Sheba, if you gain just one pound or I live to get much older, we'll both be going down on this maneuver." No doubt this maneuver was one of the things that kept this oldster so strong for her age. Dorothy rearranged the wiry-haired dog until she held Sheba's head over her shoulder, as though she was going to burp her. "There now. Don't act too stunned when you see Maggie, okay?" she whispered in Sheba's cocked ear.

"Howdy, Dearest Dorothy," Earl said smack up against the back of Dorothy's head.

"Earl!" Dorothy yelped as she turned to face him. "How many times do I have to tell you to announce your arrival, please! Why, I nearly launched Sheba!"

Earl was always excited about seeing Dorothy. Ever since early that afternoon when his mother told him the Hookers were coming to their house, Earl had been watching for her. No sooner was May Belle's announcement out of her mouth than he went directly to the front closet, pulled on his spring jacket and flung open the door.

"Earl!" May Belle called after him. "The ladies aren't coming until after dinner, honey."

"That's all right, Mother. Dearest Dorothy might come early. I just don't want her to miss our house. I better wait out front on the porch so she sees me."

"For goodness sakes, Earl. Dorothy knows where we live. She knows where *you* live, Earl. It's too early to start watching. You'll lock up your eyes, staring down the road for six hours."

May Belle's short, portly figure was framed by the archway that led from the dining room into the living room of her house, which had been built around 1900. She held a wooden spoon covered with frosting in her right hand while wiping the left on her ruffly blue apron. Earl stood holding the screen door open with his back. With both hands, he tugged his Cubs baseball cap tightly down on his head, completely shading his eyes. Mother and son stood frozen, staring at one another for a moment.

Earl often appeared to May Belle stunningly like Homer, aside from her blue-gray eyes. Same square jaw as his father. Same nose. Same thickness, height and rounded-shoulder posture. This was one of those moments. As powerfully as she loved her son, she missed her husband, even though she had been a widow for many years.

After a few seconds, she began waving the spoon back and forth as though to wipe away her thought. Then she began waving it at Earl.

"Earl Justice, come on in now and close that door. You won't miss our Dearest Dorothy. You can wait on the porch after dinner. In the meantime, get in the kitchen. I've got a few things I need you to do to help us get ready for tonight, and I've got a sinkful of spoons and bowls just waitin' to be licked." May Belle knew how to persuade her beloved Earl.

But now spoon licking and dinner were over and his Dearest Dorothy had finally arrived. He followed close behind her, right up the front steps and into the house, repeatedly and intermittently apologizing for scaring her and loudly announcing her arrival.

"Apologies accepted, Earl. You know I can't stay mad at you for even a minute. And where's your mother? And is Maggie here yet?" Maggie only lived a few doors down from May Belle.

"Mother's in the kitchen, Dearest Dorothy. She's been cleaning and cooking all day," Earl said. "I haven't seen Miss Maggie." He always called everyone Miss or Mr. whatever his or her first name was, aside from Dorothy. She was special. When Earl was beginning to talk, Dorothy had plopped down on May Belle's porch swing, drawn him up in her lap, nestled the top of his head under her chin and begun to sing "Casey Jones." Earl, who ordinarily didn't take to anyone not immediate family, softened his little body and melted right into her.

"Oh, my," May Belle had said as she watched this heart-warming sight. "He sure loves his Dearest Dorothy." Earl had smiled and repeated "Dearest Dorothy," and the name had stuck with the Justice family—and a good number of other Partonville friends—ever since. It just seemed to fit.

Dorothy passed Sheba off to Earl and set her handbag down on one of the head chairs at the dining room table, reserving the prime spot. Then she helped herself to a chocolate-covered raisin out of the bridge mix piled in a cut glass bowl neatly centered on a bright yellow floral napkin.

Dorothy gave the table a quick once-over while she chewed, then picked through the bridge mix for another chocolate-covered raisin. Everything was set up just so for the evening's game of bunco: score pads; pencils; two sets of three dice, one set at each end of the table; coasters for the glasses; and, of course, four bowls of bridge mix. Although the Happy Hookers had, aside from Nellie Ruth, long ago stopped hooking rugs together and taken up bunco, no one was willing to let go of their dangerous name. The club had ended its rug hooking thirty-three years ago, the day Dorothy, in a dramatic presentation, shouted, "Bore, bore, BORE," then threw her half-hooked rug and all materials off her lap and into her bag, where it remained until she finally donated the entire lot to the thrift shop.

Earl gave Sheba a couple quick head pats, then set her

down. She made a beeline for the kitchen, skidding to a halt on the green-and-white linoleum floor right in front of May Belle. May Belle always had a goodie waiting for Sheba, and Sheba never missed a trick.

"How's my little darlin'?" May Belle asked, then tossed Sheba a piece of liver sausage held out from lunch just for this purpose. Sheba jumped up on her hind legs and snapped it out of the air. "Do you know you enter a room about like The Tank enters Partonville?" May Belle laughed at her own joke. Dorothy heard the wisecrack just before she turned into the kitchen, still chewing.

"Well, that's a fine howdy do after that grand birthday lunch yesterday!" Dorothy quipped. "You'd think you were happier to see Sheba than me! And don't be picking on my driving, or you can drive yourself to our next hair appointment." May Belle, who never mustered the courage to learn to drive, just grinned at her friend, knowing full well she was pulling her leg, especially since May Belle always enjoyed walking the few blocks to the shop, whether it was nine or ninety degrees.

"The table sure looks great. And I feel real lucky tonight," Dorothy said as she sauntered across the room to the kitchen table, where the dessert cake was sitting on May Belle's beautiful, Imperial Candlewick cake plate. Like a teasing child, Dorothy first ran her little finger across the top of the bumpy glass edging before lightly letting it rim into the frosting, right where the cake met the platter. She scooped May Belle's buttery confectioner's sugar frosting right into her mouth.

"Hey! That'll be enough of THAT!" May Belle yelped.

"Why leave a cake sitting where we can see it if you don't want us to eat it?"

"Dorothy Jean Wetstra. You'd think after eighty-some-odd years of friendship I'd have better sense than to leave a cake out in front of *you*!"

"Sense has never been your strong point, dearie. But cake-making sure has." Dorothy licked her finger to make sure she hadn't missed a morsel of sweetness. "What do ya say we skip bunco tonight and just go right to dessert?"

Before May Belle had a chance to answer, Earl announced that Miss Gladys and Miss Jessie had arrived. Gladys McKern was Partonville's ten-month acting mayor. Many still wondered if her installation was legal. "Could they just declare a wife mayor to finish her deceased husband's term like that?" they buzzed when Gladys wasn't around. Thus, she was hardly ever referred to as anything short of Acting Mayor Gladys McKern, lest anyone mistakenly think she'd been elected. Jessie Landers was known around town for a lot of things, including hanging in there all these years as Arthur's wife ("How *does* she put up with that cantankerous husband of hers?" was muttered on more than one occasion), but mostly for making her mark as a Partonville star when she played semi-professional softball in her heyday. She and Gladys nearly knocked Earl and each other over getting into the kitchen to see if Maggie was there.

"No, she's not here yet." Dorothy figured she would just beat them to the question. Sheba ran between Gladys and Jessie, greedily collecting scratches and compliments.

"Miss Nellie Ruth's here!" Earl hollered from the living room.

"Great," May Belle said. "Just show her in, Earl."

At sixty-two, Nellie Ruth McGregor was the youngest of the six remaining Hookers; Edna and Rose had long been deceased, and no one had come along to replace them. Although Gladys had once recommended that Cora Davis be invited in, the rest of the club vetoed her suggestion, fearing that every word they shared would make the rounds. The girls had simply learned how to create their own version of bunco with six instead of eight, each pretty much playing for herself rather than in teams, the way it was usually done.

Finally, everyone had arrived but Maggie. Just when the ladies were getting on quite the collective chit chatty roll about the latest goings-on and their personal Maggie Malone speculations, in she strolled, making her grand entrance with a loud "Ta Da!" She was dressed in an orange, swishy gauze skirt and top with a two-inch-wide leopard print belt. Her jet black shoulder-length locks (dyed that way, of course; no one knew what color her natural hair was, since they hadn't seen it natural since she was about sixteen) were in an updo, with sprigs of stiff hair jutting up and out of the center like a firecracker in mid-explosion. Between the hair and neckline she was adorned with deep brown eye shadow, lots of black mascara, tangerine blush and frosty orange lipstick.

"Weeell?" she uttered in a slow, dramatic drawl. Although she stood center kitchen, hip cocked and arms up and out, not one of them could figure what was new. She looked, to all of them, perfectly normal for Maggie.

"Well?" she repeated louder, sounding a bit impatient.

"Well," Gladys finally responded, "you look beautiful as ever. How was the conference?"

Maggie's hands dropped to her waist and she let out a big sigh. "It was exciting and . . . and . . . painful." She jutted her right leg out in front of her, toe pointed and lightly touching the floor. Then Nellie Ruth made the discovery.

"Oh, my gosh," she whispered. "OH, my GOSH!" she yelped. "Maggie's got a TATTOO!"

Maggie just stood there, beaming from ear to ear, while the ladies all but stormed her trying to see exactly where and what while speaking those same curiosities aloud. If only Harold Crabb, editor of the *Partonville Press*, had known about this photo opportunity! The flurry of activity and squealing voices caused Sheba to burst into fits of barking. The kitchen so quickly turned into chaos that even Earl, who really didn't much like crowds, came roaring in from the front porch, where he had continued to wait, even though all the Happy Hookers had arrived. There stood Maggie, leaning back for balance into Gladys's arms. Nellie Ruth, who was kneeling down and holding up Maggie's right leg to get a closer look at the tattoo, began hoisting the ankle upward to give Jessie a better view. Dorothy was behind Nellie Ruth, leaning on her shoulders for balance while trying to get a look-see. May Belle was doubled over with laughter taking in this sight. They looked like a pile of elderly cheerleaders whose pyramid had tumbled down.

After trying to view the tattoo every which way, Dorothy, always being the most direct, said, "What the heck *is* it anyway?"

"Why, it's the new logo for my shop!" Maggie shrieked. "See? See the open scissors here are upside down." She twisted herself around and pointed out the details. "And they create the letter A in SPA! It's so obvious!"

Dorothy grinned when she saw Nellie Ruth's head bow and eyes slam shut. Dorothy knew Nellie Ruth well enough to know she'd begun yet more of her ongoing silent prayers for Maggie, not only for Maggie's immediate shocking behavior, but also for the very salvation of her yet unsaved soul. No, there was nothing United Methodist about a tattoo, and for all things, Nellie Ruth prayed.

"What did Ben say?" Nellie Ruth asked when the group had quieted down. Ben was Maggie's husband of fifty-two years and the love of her life.

"Truth is, he doesn't even know about it yet." Eyebrows throughout the entire room raised in a salute to this startling piece of information. "I told him when I phoned from Chicago this morning that I'd probably just make it home in time to park the car and run over to May Belle's for the meeting. And that's just what I did. All he's seen of me since I returned is a twirl of my skirt when I ran in, gave him my 'Hi, honey' kiss and headed back out the door."

"Oh, my!" Nellie Ruth smacked her hands to her cheeks and said, "Oh, my!"

3

It was nearly 10:00 P.M., an hour past most of their bed-times, aside from Maggie, who was the latest of late-night owls. The excitement of Maggie's shocking adventure and all the chatter, explanations and exclamations immediately following had backed up their playing time by nearly ninety minutes. By the time they finally moved off the topic of tattoos, heard all the details about Maggie's hotel room and the latest styles and products, there was barely time for bunco before Dorothy started hinting that surely it must be cake time.

Even though they got in only two rounds, hardly enough to qualify for prizes, May Belle had Earl hand them out anyway. He was nodding off in a kitchen chair, but he always loved being the bearer of gifts, and May Belle knew that after all these years he'd be very disappointed—and so would the gals—if he missed this special duty. There were prizes for most wins, most buncos and a booby prize, given respectively to Maggie, Jessie and Gladys. It wasn't Dorothy's lucky evening after all. Each winner received a proportionate assortment of May Belle's homemade cookies, wrapped in clear plastic wrap, secured by loops of multicolored ribbons. Everyone was too full to unwrap them, which is just the way May Belle liked it: full bellies on the way out the door and plenty to enjoy tomorrow. The last of the decaf coffee was poured and most had settled back in their chairs when the conversation shifted.

"You all heard about Tess Walker, right?" Nellie Ruth asked.

"Yes," Jessie said, "Cora Davis phoned to tell me."

"She phoned me, too," said May Belle.

Everyone else acknowledged hearing about it from one person or the other, but mostly they'd heard from Cora Davis, Partonville's unofficial town crier. Even her husband called her that on occasion.

"Why is the funeral being held so long after her death? My goodness, she dies on Friday and doesn't get buried until a week later?" Nellie Ruth wondered aloud.

Gladys responded, "There's only one relative left in the family, her sister's daughter Katie, and she lives in Chicago. Said she just can't get arrangements made until then. She's been talking to Eugene." Eugene Casey was the owner and undertaker at Casey's Funeral Home, Partonville's one and only facility for FINAL RESTING PLACE PREPARATIONS, as it said on his sign. Although there were two cemeteries, Eugene was the only one who actually buried anyone in them.

"I didn't know Tess very well. I'm sure I'm not the only one," Jessie said.

"I used to spend my fair share of time with her," Dorothy said, "especially when we were in our late teens and early twenties. Used to have quite the time together, in fact. May Belle and I were talking about this yesterday. She and her younger sister, Clarice, used to come out to the farm, and we'd berry-pick along the creek. Lively girls, those two sisters, and nearly inseparable. Of course, there was never a berry in our basket by the time we returned. Just lots of purple fingers and tongues!" Dorothy laughed at the memory.

Rather than laughing, Jessie looked surprised, then asked, "You mean Tess was normal once?"

"Of *course* she was normal, Jessie!" Dorothy responded. "I'm not sure she wasn't normal, whatever that is anyway, right up to the end. And are any of *us* really normal?" Dorothy paused and glanced around the room, her twinkling, challenging eyes landing on each one of them. Not an argument was rendered, although a few shoulders shrugged. "Tess was just lost after her sister moved to Chicago so suddenly. It shattered her. I remember her telling me right after Clarice left that it felt like a piece of *herself* backed out of that driveway on Vine Street when her sister pulled away, all her belongings crammed into that little car."

"It's surprising they were so close, with that big age difference and all," Nellie Ruth said.

"Well," Dorothy responded after gathering her thoughts for a moment, "their mom died when Tess was only about seventeen, and their dad had died years before in a combine accident, so that left Tess pretty much devoting her life to raising her baby sister. They became bonded on many levels—sister to sister, mother to daughter, what with that fifteen-year age gap. . . . After Clarice's death, Tess's lifeline shriveled up. She got so she wouldn't answer the door for anyone besides Wilbur when he delivered groceries from Your Store. I always asked him to pass along my greetings to her, especially after she stopped answering her phone. He said she did write her own checks, from what he could tell. Obviously she was at least engaged with life enough to take care of her finances.

"The one thing I regret most is not going ahead and getting folks together from the church to at least care for her yard. Yes," Dorothy said in a thoughtful voice, "I regret that very much." She lowered her head and stared for a moment at her entwined fingers resting in her lap.

"Me, too," May Belle whispered.

"Well, I heard the entire inside of her house is such a ramshackle that the paramedics could barely get the gurney through!" Gladys's loud, unsympathetic voice broke the silence. She, being the acting mayor, seemed always to be privy to insider information—something that really rattled Cora Davis! "I've wondered if I shouldn't have a look-see myself, just in case I'd need to get the health department to condemn it or something. That place has been so grown up with weeds for so long that it would be a great beautification to Partonville just to have the entire lot, house and all, bulldozed. I mean, where HAS that Chicago niece been all this time, what with Tess being her mother's only sister?"

"For goodness sakes, Gladys! Don't you think you're getting a bit carried away here?" What Dorothy wanted to say but was checked from doing so by her spiritual side was that Gladys had grown a little too power-hungry since her installation.

"I'm just telling you that there are comments in official documents leading me to believe I might have to get involved, like it or not."

Speculations soon died out as everyone started yawning and could feel the evening coming to a close. It had been a big evening indeed. Jessie nominated it to go down in the club's "Best of Happy Hookers Moments" they shared each year during the Christmas gathering that, since the club's inception, took place out at Dorothy's farm. Dorothy's two sons and her grandkids always flew in for the holidays; her daughter was deceased. Many others from Partonville, whether in or out of the club, were naturally invited to the gala. Dorothy could accommodate quite the crowd in her big old farmhouse, and she had always loved entertaining. Sometimes there were upwards of sixty people at the Christmas party, filling nearly every nook and cranny of her inviting and fully greeneried-for-the-occasion homestead. All the kids, grandkids and now great-grandkids played board games together and ran around bumping into one another while the adults chattered and laughed and ate themselves silly.

"Yup," Jessie said, "although the entire town will probably be talking about this evening within two days, we'll have to give it a blow-by-blow rehash at the Christmas party when everyone's together so they can for once hear the same version!" Everyone chuckled. Everyone but Dorothy, that is. A flicker of sadness crossed her face. But whatever thought had captured her, it only lasted a moment before the mass exit began.

One by one the Hookers said their good-byes and thanked May Belle. Earl had slipped off to bed right after passing out the prizes. May Belle and Dorothy stood together on the front porch, waving.

"Jessie," Dorothy called out to her just before she got into her car, "tell Arthur I'll be bringing The Tank around sometime this week so he can fix that door properly!"

"Oh, I'm sure he'll be glad to hear *that,*" Jessie quipped as she fired up her big old Buick and headed toward the country.

Since Dorothy couldn't see well enough to drive at night—even though she never admitted it—she'd stuffed her pj's, toothbrush and Bible in her giant handbag, knowing the Hookers' evenings usually ran late.

"Whew," May Belle said as she closed the door and slid the deadbolt until it locked into place.

"Whew exactly," Dorothy said. She plopped herself down on the couch like a rag doll, then patted her knee for Sheba to come sit in her lap. "Think we oughta wait up and watch out the front window to make sure we don't see Maggie tromping down the street with her suitcase?"

"Nope," May Belle said. "I imagine that after all these years Ben isn't shocked by much Maggie does."

Dorothy nodded her head in agreement. Sheba sat perched on the end of her leg, head hanging down over her knee. Dorothy repeatedly ran her right hand between Sheba's ears. "Lot of excitement for us old gals, wasn't it, dearie? I imagine you're as pooped as we are." Sheba didn't move her head, but her ears cocked back to acknowledge she knew she was being spoken to.

May Belle removed her apron and hung it on the bentwood hat rack next to Earl's ball cap. She then seated herself across from Dorothy in her favorite green wing chair with hand-crocheted doilies on the arms. She studied her friend's face for some time as they sat in silence. May Belle contemplated the fact that somewhere during the evening Dorothy had lost her spunk. She couldn't help but wonder what had caused it. One thing, since she'd known Dorothy nearly all her life, she knew Maggie's tattoo wouldn't be the kind of thing to rattle her. Nope, she figured Dorothy'd have her usual comment about that: "To each his own, and we're each owned by the same loving Father." It seemed to May Belle that Dorothy started getting quiet after the conversation about the Christmas party.

"You okay, old friend?"

"Yup. Just tired."

"So what do you really think of Maggie's latest adventure?"

"To each his own, and we're each owned by the same loving Father. One day Maggie will know that, too, just like you and I do. And goodness knows Nellie Ruth's sayin' prayers for her right now! Yup, we each gotta make our own decisions." She stopped stroking Sheba and rested her hand on the crook of her back. Her eyes never lifted and her expression revealed she was far off in thought. They sat in silence for a few minutes, then May Belle, still wondering what was bothering her best friend but trusting that Dorothy and the Lord would work it out, finally got up and turned on the hall light before turning off the floor lamps.

"Time to hit the sack, as Homer used to say." May Belle waited for Dorothy to signal Sheba and head for her bedroom. "Your room reservation is the first door to your left, madam."

"Ah, my usual." Dorothy patted May Belle on the back as these two white-haired old friends—one tall and dressed in pink, the other nearly a foot shorter and wearing a faded-blue gingham housedress—walked silently side by side down the hall, Sheba close behind. Then they parted ways, each into her own room.

Sheba jumped up on the end of the twin bed and curled up in a circle before Dorothy had even flipped on the ceiling light. She unzipped the giant bag and laid out her pink, one hundred percent cotton, long-legged pajamas. Next she set her worn, burgundy leather Bible, name engraved on it in faded gold print, on the nightstand beside the bed and touched the lamp shade that turned on the light. *Just like in the commercials,* she thought. "Could the Clapper be far behind?" she asked Sheba aloud to no response. She pulled out her brush and ran it through her hair a few times. Rummaging for the plastic bag containing her toothbrush, toothpaste and plate container, she walked to the bathroom.

When she reentered the bedroom, she turned off the ceiling light and changed into her pj's, carefully draping her clothes on the corner ladder-back chair. She whopped the pillows a couple good ones, folded down the bedspread just short of Sheba, then slid under the sheet and worn quilt. Turning to the Psalms, her ritual evening "Moment with the Big Guy," as she liked to refer to it, Dorothy silently read the words of Psalm 139, lips moving to each word. She needed to be reminded and dwell in the knowledge that God knew all there was to know about her. All.

"O Lord, Thou hast searched me and known me. Thou dost know when I sit down and when I rise up; Thou dost understand my thought from afar. . . ."

She read it through twice before turning off the light.

The Tank was bedded down for the night, allowing Partonville's citizens and the surrounding farmers to rest easy. Dorothy wasn't sure if she would, however. After all, like Maggie, she had her own decisions to make.

"Dear Lord," she prayed, "give me answers. Now. Amen."

4

It was eleven-thirty. Sunday night, and forty-seven-year-old Katie Durbin was sitting very erect at the kitchen table, papers stacked up in front of her in neat piles. She had shuffled and rearranged them until she thought her head was going to burst. CNN news blared from the television in the background, and the Braun was empty of its last drop of French vanilla coffee. One of her steadfast rules was no caffeine after 4:30 P.M. She was angry with herself for this lapse; her nerves were already stretched to the max.

Surely, she'd thought when she first received the phone call from the hospital in Partonville early last Friday morning, surely there had to be another relative. Another way. Something or someone who could relieve her of this nightmare. But nothing in her mother's documents that she'd just finished prowling through proved otherwise: she was the only living relative of Tess Walker, her deceased mother's sister. Yes, Tess was her aunt, but she'd rather not have to admit that either backward Partonville or any of its residents, especially one strange and peculiar duck, was remotely related to her. Now not only did she have to admit it, albeit thankfully not to anyone in her circle of friends, but she also had to see to it that Aunt Tess got buried on Thursday.

She sat tapping her Mont Blanc pen on the table with

her right hand while running the spread fingers of her left hand through her hair. A couple loose strands stuck in her cocktail ring between the platinum setting and the sapphire. She squinted up her face as she yanked the hairs right out of her scalp. Revealing evidence of pain wasn't her style, but who was looking now anyway?

"Great!" she spat as she pulled the hairs from her ring and inspected them. "On top of everything else I need my roots done, and my appointment is Thursday!" About three-eighths of an inch of speckles of gray appeared at the scalp end of one of the deep red strands. She continued muttering out loud to no one. "Maybe Jeffrey can squeeze me in tomorrow."

"Mom," Josh said, "are you talking to yourself now?" At fifteen, Joshua Matthew Kinney, Katie's only child from her long-ago failed marriage, wandered over to the refrigerator, swung open the door, stood staring into it for a moment, then grabbed the milk, unscrewed the lid and took a few swigs while holding the door open.

"Josh!"

"I know. Don't hold the door open. Don't drink out of the milk container. Shouldn't you be in bed?"

"Well, if you know the drill, why . . ." Her voice trailed off as she shook her head, clunked her elbows down on the table and cradled her temples in her hands.

Josh silently retreated back to his room, turned off the computer and crawled into bed. He lay there on his back for quite some time, eyes open, staring into the darkness, listening to the sounds of news blaring under his bedroom door in their perfectly remodeled Lincoln Park brownstone.

She could make things perfect on the outside, he thought, but she sure couldn't seem to hide her own internal disaster at the moment. He wondered if his mom might just finally be cracking. Perhaps she was human after all.

He recalled her events of the last week. Fender bender with the Lexus on Wednesday. Canned from her vice-president job with the real estate development firm on Thursday. And then, the call from Partonville on Friday. Oddly, that seemed to be the most distressing to her. Not that her aunt had died, but that she had to do something about it. He felt that he didn't really know his mom at all, nor did she seem to care to know him. This was just one more thing he could wonder about, but not anymore tonight. He finally rolled on his side, punched his pillow a couple times to fluff it under his cheek, then closed his eyes. In two days he would finally get to see this "backward and pathetic Partonville" place his mother moaned about.

Katie rinsed out the coffeepot, then reviewed her notes and checklist. She had spoken with the coroner, had the body picked up from the hospital and talked about burial. She decided cremation was the route to go since Aunt Tess didn't have a plot. She would have skipped a wake and funeral altogether if she hadn't been talked out of it by the pastor. The only details left concerning the arrangements were ordering flowers and meeting with him on Wednesday. What in the world kind of flowers should she get for a crazy aunt she really didn't know and hadn't seen for more than a decade? What could she even say on the card? *For goodness sake, no one will read it anyway!*

No sooner did she have that thought than she dismissed it. Of course people would attend the funeral and go around reading all the cards. What else did they have to do in Partonville? At least Pastor Delbert Carol, Jr., at the United Methodist Church had sounded more normal on the phone than that Eugene Casey at Casey's Funeral Home! He nearly drove Katie crazy trying to get her to have the funeral on Tuesday. No way could she pull that off. Pastor, however, told her not to worry, that he would help her put the details together. He said he'd talk to Eugene and coordinate things. *One step at a time. I'll worry about Aunt Tess's house later. One thing at a time.*

Katie sifted through one of the stacks and found the photo she'd intentionally buried at the bottom. It was a black and white of her mom and Aunt Tess. They were standing next to a silo, arms around one another's shoulders, laughing. Her mom looked to be in her early twenties. She studied it, curious about the location, guessing it was taken before her mom moved to Chicago. Before her mom met her dad, thus before Katie was born. She looked first at the face of her mother, then at Aunt Tess. It always startled her that she could never see a family resemblance. Her mother didn't look like her sister, and she herself looked like neither of them. Katie's father had died before she was born, and there wasn't a single photo of him to be found. Although her mother said she had his eyes, no evidence could physically prove it. Even her dad's folks had been killed in an auto accident when he was only seven.

She began wishing her mother were here. She would know how to deal with funeral arrangements and churches. Katie hadn't stepped inside a church or ventured back to Partonville since her mother died. The only reason she'd occasionally gone to church the decade before that was to please her mother, who said she prayed for Katie every day. When Katie's worst fears were realized and she learned her husband had been cheating on her, she determined right then and there that prayers were for the weak ones and God didn't answer them anyway, if there even was a God. Yes, she wished her mom were here, not only because she'd know how to deal with church, but because she'd know how to deal with Partonville, since those were *her* roots. Katie, gratefully, was one hundred percent a city girl.

Suddenly her eyes began to sting and a knot formed in her stomach. Must be the caffeine, she concluded. She slid the photo back in its hidden place, remembering why she had put it there in the first place—*emotional rides are for the weak ones, too*—then stacked up the piles, setting her checklist on top. She slowly got up out of the chair, which she'd been sitting in for way too long. Before turning out the kitchen light, she added one more item to her checklist and she made it number one: "Phone Gregory's FIRST THING." Gregory's was the poshest salon in Chicago, and Jeffrey, her colorist, would work at nothing less. Odds of actually getting a color appointment moved this late in the game were slim to none. But she wasn't one to play the odds. She was one to get her way. That is, until recently, it seemed.

At 6:00 A.M. Katie was up prowling through her library of exercise videos. She still had three hours to wait before she could call the salon. She hadn't slept well, and her entire body felt stiff and old. What would it be today? Cardiovascular workout? Yoga? Kickboxing? In an attempt to drown out the craziness in her head, she settled on a routine that was one of her least favorites but that had bouncy music from the sixties. She popped the cassette into the VCR and

pushed the button. While she one-and-twoed it along with
the instructor, her thoughts raced between funeral arrangements and her career.

Although she had been blindsided by her sudden dismissal, she was very aware it had been precipitated by her
number one rival's power play to dethrone her and capture
her job. The risks and cutthroat competition in industrial
and residential development could be brutal, but then
that's the way she liked to play the game herself. That's why
from the get-go she'd introduced herself and signed all official papers as Kathryn C. Durbin, a name with distinction,
rather than her humiliating given name of Katie Mabel
Carol Durbin. What in the world was her mother thinking
anyway, giving her a name that sounded so . . . Partonville!
The fact that she grew up hating getting her fingernails
dirty, drove a pricey SUV rather than a pickup and preferred the opera and gallery openings to corncribs and coy-
otes made her given name all the more ridiculous. Her
mom had told her that Mabel was a strong name and that
her dad had come up with Carol. Katie just groaned when
she heard the explanation. She hated her name so much
that she'd never even told her son the whole of it.

Katie was mildly embarrassed about her dismissal, but
she wasn't worried about finances or her ability to bounce
back. In fact, she didn't have to worry about money at all;
between her severance, her gutsy real estate takeovers in the
last eight years and her prudent stock market investments,
she wouldn't have to work another day in her life. It's just
that she loved the hunt. In fact, she was already planning
how to position herself against Keith Benton, the guy who
had caused her temporary fall. Strong, Hart and Cleaver
had, for quite some time, been trying to lure her away any-

way. She would undoubtedly move one more rung up the success ladder if she accepted their offer. Maybe she would become a full partner in the conglomerate before the year was out.

But first, first she'd have to deal with Partonville.

"Mom, do you think you can turn that TV down?" Josh's auburn hair was askew and his sweatpants were wrinkled from a night's tossing and turning. His five-foot-ten-inch self stood staring daggers at his mother, who was tirelessly bouncing up and down, red hair dancing atop her head, five-foot-five-inch slender frame looking like a pogo stick on speed. How, he wondered, could anyone be so determined so early in the morning.

"Just five more minutes, Josh. My workout will end in five more minutes. You have to get up soon anyway," she said somewhat breathlessly between hops.

"Oh, right. Like I'm not up already."

"Josh, don't use that tone of voice with me," she said as the video moved into its slow-down portion before coming to an end.

"You did phone Latin, right?"

Katie felt a stab of guilt as once again, in the midst of her busy life, she'd dropped the ball handling something for her son. The Latin School of Chicago was the oldest independent school in the city and certainly among the most prestigious and expensive. Although Josh was neither a jock, the artsy type nor a pocket protector kind of guy—in fact, he had yet to discover his "type"—he had been forced by his mother into attending Latin when he would have much preferred the public school near their home. She insisted he get an education at Latin, believing upper status and "rigorous college preparatory education," as it said in the brochure, would set him up to be a top-notch whatever it was he'd decide to be.

Well, top-notch wasn't his goal if it meant ending up like her. And he might as well add his dad to that mix, too. Dad had become much more concerned with his second marriage's "Daily Kids," as Josh secretly referred to them, than with Josh. All either of his parents ever wanted to know, it seemed, was "Are you applying yourself?" Other than that, he was at the bottom of their lists.

"Mom. You did call them, didn't you?" He'd read the look on his mother's face that let him know she hadn't.

"It's on my list for today. We're not leaving until tomorrow anyway, Josh. Don't worry so much."

Right.

5

At 5:45 A.M. Wednesday, Arthur Landers parked his 1993 Ford pickup outside Harry's Grill on the Partonville square, turned off the engine and sat behind the wheel staring at the CLOSED sign on the front door. Harry's was the only grill in town and one of the few true greasy spoons left in the county. Even so, Lester would not unlock that door until exactly the crack of 6:00 A.M., no exceptions. Not weather, emergency or complaining could make him change his routine. And he closed at 6:00 P.M. Sharp. Even if a friend was trying to get in to join another, "Too dang bad. Shoulda got here on time." Twist goes the lock in the door. End of story.

Arthur, Jessie's husband for fifty-nine less-than-blissful years and the only mechanic who'd ever worked on The Tank, wasn't much for patience, other than when he was wielding a wrench under the hood of a car. Then there was no end to it. It was the challenge and dance between steel and man that he enjoyed. But for now, he sat in his truck staring at the door to Harry's. If looks could vaporize, all but his steaming coffee would have disintegrated by now.

At five-fifty, Acting Mayor Gladys McKern bustled her way to be first in line, as usual. Heaven forbid Partonville's Queen Lady, as Arthur liked to refer to her, should miss an opportunity to be first. She was immediately followed by Eugene Casey, Harold Crabb, Pastor Delbert and the rest of the regulars. Of this six-day-a-week order of events he could be assured.

Arthur considered this eclectic group, although *eclectic* was a word clearly out of the realm of his vocabulary. They were lined up practically right in front of his bumper. Occasionally, just to get everyone's juices running, he'd roll down his window and spit. Why, sometimes he even cranked over his engine, just to see them jump. Then he'd grin like a fool. It's not that he was a mean person; determined and set in his ways, like Lester, would be more like it. And he definitely enjoyed being an instigator.

Finally, Lester turned the key, flipped the CLOSED sign to OPEN and the swarm entered. Steaming cups of coffee were already waiting at each unofficially designated place. Lester knew who had decaf and who didn't. Who used cream and who took extra sugar. Like Santa Claus on the night before Christmas, Lester spoke not a word but kept straight to his work as the customers plunked onto their stools. Mostly they saw Lester's back, since the grill was located at the end of the U, although they all knew he never missed a word.

Lester had biscuits and sausage gravy and eggs over easy to cook and serve. And this being Wednesday, he had bacon and onions to cook up for the liver special, and spuds to peel for his famous "smashed taters," as they were listed on his hand-scrawled and photocopied menus in plastic page protectors. No time to chat for Lester. No sooner would he be done with breakfast than the lunch crowd would begin arriving at 10:30 A.M. Farmers got hungry early. Then right on into the early supper crowd so he could lock that door at six o'clock, try to get people to hurry and finish up, clean up the grill and head home to his bachelor dwelling by seven.

"Harold," Gladys hollered across the counter, "any news I ought to know about this morning?"

"None that I can think of. Some more garbage cans were smashed, but that's about it," he said without raising his head from his magazine.

"Nothing more on Tess Walker's state of affairs?"

"Like what?" Suddenly Harold stopped looking at his fishing magazine and gave full attention to Gladys. Perhaps she knew something that he ought to know.

"Like have you asked for official reporter's permission to inspect that place?"

"For what?"

"For possible condemnation."

"Gladys, it's my understanding that her next of kin hasn't even had a chance to look. Why should I? No crime has been committed. And whatever could lead you to believe it needs to be condemned? Just because someone lets her lawn grow tall enough to be baled rather than mowed doesn't mean her place ought to be condemned." He stuck his head back in his magazine at the end of that sentence, trying to dismiss her.

Now it was Arthur's turn. "There's always a farmer looking for hay," he said, looking at Gladys. "Think Tess's yard is big enough to get baling equipment in?" Arthur chuckled, having obviously pleased himself with that one.

"Oh, Arthur." Gladys was clearly disgusted no one was taking her seriously. As if on cue and making a social commentary, BANG! Lester thunked down her plate of "two-poached-eggs-no-bacon-rye-toast-with-no-butter-doc-says-I-gotta-watch-my-cholesterol" order, which always came out of her mouth in one breath. The disruption to her thoughts startled her and caused her to give him a good stare. He returned Gladys's look of disgust, crunched eyebrow to crunched eyebrow, and she thought she saw him shake his head when he turned back toward the grill. This didn't stop Gladys from finishing the diatribe she'd started at bunco last night.

"I'm just saying that I read in official documents that they could barely get the gurney through, her place was so piled up with stuff."

"Everyone's got a right to be messy, Gladys." Harold turned the page of his magazine while Gladys looked around, seeking anyone's support but finding no takers.

She spun on her stool thirty degrees to her right, reached across the front of Arthur and grabbed two pats of butter out of the bowl in front of him. She proceeded to unwrap the little foils and spread every last drop of butter onto her toast, scraping the foil with her knife for any remaining signs of cholesterol. Eugene watched her, then shot Lester a glance as Lester slammed Eugene's biscuits and gravy down in front of him. Lester again shook his head back and forth, Gladys's inconsistency having been fully visible to him as well. Same every morning.

"Got any *real* news on that developer I heard has been snooping around our parts?" Arthur asked Harold. Gladys sounded a loud "hmph."

"Nothing official, but I'm hoping to have more infor-mation by Sunday's edition. I sent Sharon over to Hethrow this morning to try and get an interview with anyone from Craig & Craig. From what I've heard, several people have seen one of their red pickup trucks driving in your neck of the woods, Arthur. Seen anything of them?"

"Nope. Can't say that I have." If Arthur had seen them, he probably wouldn't tell Harold anyway. He much preferred talking to that sassy little Sharon Teller. She was as cute as a bug.

"What make trucks are they drivin'?" Arthur asked.

"Toyotas."

"Traitors. I hope they go broke in a hurry." Arthur had definite opinions about foreign cars and the people who bought them. Just wasn't American.

"I can't think of anyone who would sell his home and land at any price on that east side, no matter how much they offered," Harold said. "And that's the kind of information I hope Sharon can come up with, names—although I doubt she'll be able to. Developers always hold their cards close to their vests. So far we've got nothing but talk. But the amount of talk is increasing. Something must be in the wind."

Cora Davis arrived and settled into her usual table at the window. Then they all turned their heads simultaneously at the slam of the screen door. Earl always let it slam. He was the only one Lester allowed to get away with it without quoting the cost of a new door. He'd finally decided to give up stopping Earl from slamming the door when Earl turned twenty and it became obvious the banging just wasn't *going* to stop.

"Mornin', Earl," Lester said.

"Good morning, Mr. Lester." Earl walked around behind the counter and stood about a yard away from Lester, watching him flip eggs and smash bacon with his bacon press.

"Got any deliveries for me today, Mr. Lester?" He sounded hopeful, as he loved to be useful.

"Not 'til lunchtime, I reckon, Earl. Same as always. Come back at eleven, okay? And tell your mother howdy for me." For more than twenty years, Lester had "hired" Earl to deliver food. His pay was per delivery, not time, as occasionally Earl had a way of getting sidetracked, often-times to the back pew at United Methodist, where he re-arranged the Bibles and hymnals to his satisfaction. Lester now paid Earl fifty cents per delivery, and the people on the receiving end usually slipped him a quarter or so, too. Nearly all deliveries were to store owners on the square.

As Earl was on his way out the door, Arthur called to him. "Tell your momma I sure enjoyed the cookies Ms. Jessie brought home from bunco last night. I believe those snickerdoodles are my favorite."

"Yes, sir, Mr. Arthur. Yes, sir, I sure will. Mr. Lester?" Earl had opened the door but then stopped before exiting.

"Yes, Earl."

"Mr. Lester, what's a tattoo?"

"Well," he said, as he flipped a pancake in simultaneous motion with the swiveling of everyone's head toward Earl. "Well." His voice trailed off, and he wiped his hands on his apron to give himself time to think. "Why do you ask, Earl?"

"I heard Mother talking to Dearest Dorothy this morn-ing, and she said Miss Maggie got a tattoo. That doesn't mean she's sick, does it, Mr. Lester?"

All heads swiveled back to Lester, whose hands contin-ued to swipe mindlessly at his apron. All heads but Cora's, that is, whose eyes seemed to be permanently locked on Earl. It appeared as though her eyelids had flung up into her eye sockets like a retracting pull-down map in an old schoolhouse. Her mouth was agape, and her arm held her coffee cup frozen in midair. Gladys quickly looked from Lester to Cora, then grinned like a Cheshire cat, realizing that this would be one time when Cora hadn't scooped her, and she didn't want to miss delighting in it.

"Well, Earl," Lester said. "Well, a tattoo is just a decoration. I'm pretty sure you didn't hear your momma correctly anyway, Earl. I doubt Miss Maggie got a tattoo. Sometimes we get things confused."

"Not this time," Gladys said a little too happily, considering she didn't approve. But it was just too much fun to spill the beans to Cora Davis.

"Yes, Earl. Miss Maggie *did* get a tattoo, but I assure you she is just fine, honey," Gladys said.

Bang went the screen door.

Crash went Cora Davis's cup.

Dorothy and May Belle sat across from one another at May Belle's kitchen table. The last of the buttermilk pancakes had been scraped into Sheba's bowl, now licked spanking clean, and Sheba was checking under the table just to make sure there wasn't something else for her.

"Sorry, Sheba. Us two pigs ate every last scrap of the bacon," Dorothy said as she patted the top of Sheba's head.

"And wasn't it good bacon," May Belle said rather than asked.

"Yes. Where'd you get that anyway? Best I've had for some time."

"At Your Store. Seems like his meat market slices are thicker than they used to be. And kind of smoky flavored. I'll have to tell the powers that be we noticed the change and like it."

Dorothy had gotten up later than her typical 6:00 A.M., even though Sheba had arrived in the kitchen right on time. May Belle noticed Dorothy still didn't seem her usual cheery self. She had dark circles under her eyes and was kind of quiet, like last night.

"You got a doctor's appointment today, friend?"

"No. What makes you ask?"

"I've noticed you looking at your watch several times this morning as though you have an appointment. And you seem kind of preoccupied or something. Worried, maybe." May Belle was willing to let last night pass, but now Dorothy's somberness had gone on too long.

"No doctor appointment today, although I do have one on Friday that I better make sure I don't forget."

"Is something worrying you about your health?"

"Nope. Can't say that it is. Just got my regular appointment for prescription refills. I'm nearly out of my heart pills, and Doc Streator's nurse said he won't phone another refill over to Richardson's until I come and see him. And don't think I didn't try getting T.J. to slip me in one more refill. You'd think after four years of putting up with his shenanigans in the wind section he'd figure he owed me one."

"Dearest Dorothy, if everyone you taught or conducted in bands throughout the years owed you one, you'd be the most powerful lady in Partonville!" Both of them chuckled at that thought. And indeed, it wasn't far from the truth. Dorothy had been the band director at nearly every level school for more than forty-five years before she retired at age seventy. She was one of the few farm girls in their area who'd actually gone off to college. Partonville residents had been thrilled to have one of their own come home with such an honorable gift to give the community and one that she'd never stopped giving, in one way or another.

To this day, nearly everyone in town knew who Dorothy Jean Wetstra was. Although they most certainly remembered *her* name, she found that she couldn't keep all *their* names straight. Even though that was a great embarrassment to her, she never missed remembering what instrument they'd played, for she remembered each of them as part of the music of her years, the fruit of her teaching and the gifts in her life. She could look at them and name the instrument. Why, T.J. Winslow played nearly four entire high school years of the worst clarinet she'd ever heard. In fact, in Dorothy's opinion, he continued to be the sour note in the community band today, of which Dorothy was also a member. She played first clarinet, even though it wasn't the favorite of her multiple instruments, because, according to her, "they're weak in that section" and she remembered what that was like from the other side of the baton. Next to the Lord, music would always be her passion.

Dorothy pushed back from May Belle's table and periodically continued to look at her watch. At exactly 9:00 A.M., she announced to May Belle, Sheba and Earl, who had returned from Harry's, that it was time for The Tank to venture home so she could check her e-mail. Dorothy was always one to move with the times, aside from The Tank, that is. She was on her third computer upgrade and fourth modem, often laughing and referring to herself as the fastest old lady in Partonville. May Belle took Dorothy's impending departure as her signal to pack her up with a tray of cookies, bigger than any of the bunco prizes. She knew Dorothy had an unending sweet tooth and also that she was the world's worst baker.

Earl walked right behind Dorothy, all the way to her car. She opened the back door and set Sheba in her place, then got behind the wheel and arranged herself. When she closed the door, once again it didn't close right. She opened it up and slammed it again.

"Earl," she said, looking up at him while she fastened her seat belt, "I'm going to get this car over to Arthur Landers and have him fix it right before it plumb kills me trying to shut the door. Either that or I go flying out rounding a corner."

Earl didn't move. He took in what she said and thought about it while she turned over the engine. Then, as if he'd finally figured out the answer to a riddle, he looked first surprised, then worried, then said, "Dearest Dorothy, don't get killed, okay?"

"Oh, Earl, honey, I won't." With that she tromped on the gas and away she went. Earl stood motionless, staring down the road at the backside of The Tank long after it had disappeared around the corner.

6

Dorothy had once flipped The Tank, or rather she had been helpless to keep from doing so. The accident was caused by a "yahoo teenager," as she put it, who hadn't quite mastered the fine art of speeding on gravel and maintaining control the way she had. He'd come toward her, skidding out of control at the bend, leaving her nothing to do but hit the ditch, ultimately rolling down the slight embankment, The Tank settling on its roof, leaving Dorothy hanging like a rag doll by her seat belt. Boy, that was the talk of the week at Harry's and Maggie's, as well as news in the *Partonville Press.* "Dorothy Jean Wetstra Found Hanging," the headline read. That sure got everybody's attention, as well as won second runner-up for the most misleading headline in the tricounty area at the annual district press awards. That was one plaque that didn't hang on the Wall of Honor in Harold Crabb's office.

When Dorothy first told the story to Nellie Ruth, who came to visit her in the hospital where she was held overnight for observation, Nellie Ruth was at last certain that Dorothy indeed had a hot line to Jesus and a legion of angels that followed her everywhere. Thank goodness Dorothy had a reputation for being one of Partonville's most potent prayer warriors, especially when she unleashed what Nellie Ruth referred to as the Do Something Bazooka

Prayer. No dart prayers for Dorothy. Fast. Out loud and LOUDLY. "Just get right to the big guns and let God work," she always said. No one ever prayed more fervently, succinctly or with more faith than Dorothy. It was a good thing, most in town agreed, considering the way that woman drove. In fact, most in town prayed she'd quit driving, since she was beginning to scare them with her lead foot, not to mention her bad judgment. The Tank wore the proud battle scars to justify their concerns. There was a crevice in her rear left bumper the exact shape of the southwest light pole in the parking lot at Wal-Mart, along with scrapes and paint bruises that looked like a giant cat had been clawing on it and enough dents to make it look like she'd been in a demolition derby.

When Nellie Ruth asked Dorothy how in the world she had kept from panicking when she ended up upside down and suspended, Dorothy said she simply uttered her favorite prayer. Even though Nellie Ruth and practically everyone else in town knew what it was, Dorothy repeated it for her anyway: "Dear Jesus, Just DO something. Amen." And the fact of the matter was that He always did, and usually in quick order. That particular time the fire truck just "happened by" almost immediately. It had been heading back to the station from pumping out its hoses in a nearby field. Dorothy knew this was no accident and blew God a kiss when they arrived.

Jessie was putting clothes on the line when she noticed The Tank heading toward its home. Even though she'd never lost her twenty-twenty vision, a person could be half-blind and still know when The Tank was in motion, because it was the fastest thing around. Why in the world Dorothy needed to be getting home faster than a speeding bullet, Jessie couldn't imagine, but then at their age, neither of their bladders was what it used to be. She chalked the speeding vehicle up to a when-nature-calls episode and continued pinching clothespins onto the sheets.

Dorothy zinged on past Jessie's another half mile, then stopped short of the mailbox at the end of her lane. Her original intentions were to pull up to the mailbox, roll down the window, tug open the mailbox door, get the mail, then shoot on up to the house in time to make her appointment. Instead she felt a sudden need just to take in the beauty of the spring land. She sat staring the eighth mile up her lane, thinking about how familiar it was. As familiar as her own face in the mirror.

Dorothy Jean Brown Wetstra had been born on this farm. As the story went, it was during a blizzard on a November evening, the day before Thanksgiving, when her mother, Ethel, went into labor with what turned out to be her one and only child. One minute Ethel was peeling potatoes for tomorrow's gathering, the next she was doubled over the sink clutching the peeler in her hand while taking stock of the fact that life on the Crooked Creek Farm was about to change.

Since the lane and most country roads were drifted over, there was no way for them to get to a doctor or for one to make it to their house. Charles Brown calmly decided he'd helped bring enough farm animals into the world to figure things out as they came. Of this he assured his wife. She had every reason to trust him, since Charles was a man of his word.

At two minutes past two on Thanksgiving morning, Dorothy Jean arrived. She was greeted by the large and gentle hands of the man who would love her until he died at age eighty-two and the smile and joy of a mother who made it to sixty-two before finally succumbing to a yearlong battle with breast cancer.

Even when Dorothy married at age twenty-seven, she didn't leave the farm. Her faithful husband, Henry, had been more than willing to move in and share life with the Browns. He had been waiting for Dorothy to say yes to his many proposals, beginning before she left for college. In fact, he knew perhaps the only way to make sure he would get to see her every evening was to be sitting around the table, in the kitchen, in the house, on the property she loved. He remembered her telling him once that the fields themselves were part of the rhythm of her life and the notes she played. "My music just wouldn't be the same if I couldn't stand in a freshly plowed row of black Illinois earth or watch the sun go down over a field of golden corn," she told him as they sat in the parked car in the very spot Dorothy sat in now. Of course, in those days they parked at the end of the lane so Charles and Ethel wouldn't see them sparking.

Dorothy sat, hands gripping the steering wheel, recalling so many of those moments. All of her family had gone from Crooked Creek but her. Sheba finally hopped in the front seat, put her paws up against Dorothy's shoulder and began licking her face. "It's a lot to remember, isn't it, girl?" Sheba cocked her head, lost in her own doggie thoughts.

Just then a red Toyota truck pulled up behind them, slightly ahead of schedule.

La Feminique Hair Salon & Day Spa sat one block off the square. Maggie Malone had, at twenty years of age, purchased it from its original owner, whose husband had run off with the mail clerk at window number two. While tears and mascara ran down her face, the woman had scrawled a handmade sign that said, HUSBAND LEFT ME. SHOP FOR SALE, posted it in the window and within five minutes, Cora Davis, then Cora Wethersby, saw it and immediately ran over to Maggie's house to give her the news, knowing she'd been talking about getting a place of her own. It turned out that even busybodies have their golden moments, as this piece of timely information was a turning point in Maggie's life. Maggie barely beat another buyer to the shop, where she sealed the deal with a handshake. Ben, three years older than Maggie and owner of his own hauling company, said he would help finance her endeavor as long as she would marry him within two weeks. Two weeks to the day later, the long time couple became man and wife in a ceremony that took place in the Partonville square on the hottest day recorded in the town's history. Ben was so excited to have finally landed his beautiful Maggie that her profuse sweating appeared nothing more than "dewy drops of beauty," as he told her before he wiped her brow for their first of thousands of steamy man-and-wife kisses.

Over the decades, each time Maggie gave birth to one of

her nine children—she and Ben had *always* hoped for a baseball team's worth—or experienced an identity crisis, she closed down the shop, renamed it, remodeled it and had yet another grand reopening, advertising with dollar-off coupons in the *Partonville Press*. Even though it was always the same location with the same owner—and there were usually playpens, building blocks, crunched Cheerios and kids to walk over, most related to her kids' kids—the ladies of Partonville found these reopenings to be just as exciting as Maggie herself did. She always served some exotic snack or gourmet coffee she'd purchased from one of the many catalogs she received. Partonville just didn't sell the type of things that piqued Maggie's buying buds, so she ordered them. Never let it be said that Maggie Malone had slipped off the cutting edge of trends and fashions, even though her waistline had long ago caught up with her hips and she was often surrounded by a gaggle of great grandbabies!

Maggie pulled Cora's hair up between her fingers as she snipped across the gray locks with her scissors. Conversations at La Feminique Hair Salon & Day Spa had been shocking and lively since Maggie's first day back with that horrid tattoo, as everyone was already referring to it—everyone except Maggie. Although Maggie equally adored the energy and sounds of her family and her shop, the shop bustle seemed to hold special excitement for her this morning, the first day her new logo rode shotgun on her leg.

"So *what* did *Ben* have to say about this, Maggie?" Cora asked, after thoroughly inspecting the tattoo she'd so shockingly had to learn about secondhand. Of course, she'd made an appointment the minute she left the grill, just to check things out for herself. "Why, Alfred would probably divorce me if I'd gone and done something like that. Which, of course, I never would. But *gracious,* I still can't believe you are a tattooed lady!"

"I'll answer the Ben question first," Maggie said as she slipped her little finger under another section of Cora's hair and lifted it for the procedure. "Then we'll talk about a few of the things *you* have done, Cora Davis!"

Cora just raised an eyebrow in the mirror as she yielded her head into the hands of Maggie . . . who was holding those very sharp scissors very close to her aging-but-still-pretty-smooth skin.

"All the Hookers last night were so worried about what Ben would say and, truth is, he *loved* it! Although he'd never mentioned it before, he said he'd thought about getting one himself when he first hit midlife. He teased me a bit and said he 'outgrew' the notion but he guessed I wouldn't have a chance to do that, since it was a done deal. He said, 'Besides, at seventy-plus years of age, Mags, you're just too old to ground, honey!' We both had a good laugh trying to even picture him holding me back!"

"Does this new image mean the shop will be closing again for a face-lift? Last time you redid the shop was right after you got new caps on your teeth, remember? I'd just gotten used to it being called Sleek and Sheik when you went and changed it again. The truth is, though, I rather like this purple color. It seems to feel more relaxing in here than that last red-and-black-striped wallpaper. Besides, all your customers are getting too old for those loud colors!"

"I guess I get bored with things more easily than other people," Maggie said as she took another snip and kicked the building wad of hair out from under her. "This is about my favorite, though. I can't see me changing again for quite some time. And day spas are so *in* now!"

Maggie tilted Cora's head down and to the left, forcing Cora to talk into her own chest. "I've been meaning to ask you, Maggie, what *is* a day spa anyway? And the truth is, I'm not the only one who wants to know."

Maggie sighed, swung the chair around so Cora was facing her and said, "It's a full-service salon, Cora! Some day spas even have electrolysis, wax dips and massage therapists in them."

Cora caught her breath and said, "Do tell! And what do you have that makes it a day spa?"

Maggie twirled Cora's chair back around toward the mirror, pushed her head down again, pumped up the chair two notches and sighed loudly. "Me, Cora. I've got me."

7

It was 5:50 P.M. Wednesday when Katie and Josh neared Partonville. *Wake tomorrow, funeral day after . . . not much time to make sure everything is in place but more than enough time to endure,* Katie thought as she sped down the highway past field after field after field, not one tall building in sight.

They had traveled most of the way in silence since pulling out of their driveway nearly two hours behind schedule. Katie had fielded four business-networking calls, each time looking at the caller ID before deciding to put her purse down once again and engage in verbal battle. Although she wasn't worried about money during what she was sure was her temporary unemployment, she did want to plant as many corporate seeds as she could before heading out of town. Real estate was currently experiencing a wild seller's market, and things were hopping.

Neither she nor Josh had eaten lunch, and Josh's stomach was growling louder than the blabbing voices on the public network radio station Katie always had tuned in. He suspected, however, that she wasn't really listening, as the static was getting louder. Josh noticed his mom had been wearing kind of a glazed-over look for the last hour of their five-hour, southbound journey. He reached over and pushed the search button. Three times he pushed it, only to have it cough up three different country-western singers in midsong and a preacher ranting—at least that's the way he saw it—about "REPENTANCE," immediately followed by "SEND US YOUR MONEY!" *This guy probably has* very big hair! he thought to himself. *Man, no wonder Mom never goes to church!* Options being limited, he stuck with pitiful love songs.

"Great," he said aloud in disgust.

"Great what?"

"Great radio selections," he said with as much sarcasm as he could muster.

"So what's wrong with keeping abreast of world situations and unbiased news?" Katie asked. Obviously he was right about her being in her own world. He turned up the volume until the strains of the very sad singer nearly rattled the windows.

"Earth to Mom. You call 'and she left me for a hound dog and a new pair of boots' news? I didn't think you were paying attention, Mom. Should you even be driving?"

After about three more seconds of the bellowing singer's heartache, he punched the button with the side of his fist, turned the radio off and asked, in his best five-year-old imitation, "Are we there yet?" Simultaneously the worn WEL-COME TO PARTONVILLE sign appeared on the side of the road to their right. He looked at his mother's face to see if he could read her.

"Welcome to Pardon Me Ville," she said aloud, as she recalled that the sign was no more than about three quarters of a mile from the town square.

"What? Did you say Pardon Me Ville?"

"It's what I used to call this place."

"I've never heard you say that before."

"Amazing what forgotten memories we have locked

within us until something comes along to trigger them."
Her voice sounded far off.

"It looks exactly the same. Honestly, I don't think one
fence post has changed." After checking the rearview mirror, Katie slowed down. She glanced from side to side and
rolled down the window when she noticed the highway
ditches had just been mowed. Deeply she inhaled that fresh,
green fragrance, recalling the sound of her mother's breath
doing the exact same thing when they used to roll into
Partonville decades ago.

Josh put his window down and inhaled. "Well, Pardon
Me Ville smells pretty good."

"Yes, that is one of the few perks one can find in the
country. Make a note of this, Josh, as this might be the last
one we have for the next few days."

"Right." They both inhaled one more time before ap-
proaching the square. "So *this* is the square, huh? Pretty obvious when you get here."

"Take a good look, Josh. This is where all the action hap-
pens, if you can call it action. I'll give you a once-around
before we head down West Main Street to the motel."

Josh was fascinated by the merging ritual. All traffic, two
lanes deep, went counterclockwise around what appeared
to be a government building in the middle, and people
already on the square seemed to have the right of way.
Maybe. He noticed that the hands on the large clock pro-
truding off one of the corners of the stone building were
stopped at one-fourteen.

"No digital, huh?" Josh quipped. "Do they even have
computers here?"

"I couldn't tell you, but I imagine we'll find out when we

check into the motel and I see if their phones have computer jacks for my laptop."

"I brought mine, too. Thought I'd keep Alex posted on my nightlife now that we've entered Corn Country." He laughed at himself. "And speaking of corn, I'm starving! Nice segue, huh, Mom? Can we get something to eat before we check in? I see a sign that has a coffee cup on it. See it, there on the right just past the drugstore?"

"That would be Harry's," she said flatly, feeling her stomach lurch at the greasy memories. "Unless it's changed hands, which I doubt." She drove right on by, not even slowing for the parking place in front. "I really do want to check in first, Josh. Just to make sure we've got rooms."

Josh craned his neck as they sailed past. Indeed, it was called Harry's, and it looked pretty full. He wondered if they'd have to wait long when they returned. His stomach gave another loud growl.

Katie missed her turnoff, unable to get to the outside lane of the circle. When they were about to drive past Harry's for the second time, Josh suddenly said, "Mom, *please* can we eat first? I'm starving! And look, there's still a parking place right in front."

Katie quickly checked her rearview mirror and pulled into the parking spot, deciding to give her son a break.

"Thanks, Mom. I'm about to turn inside out from hunger."

They unbuckled their seat belts and walked toward the cafe door. Just as Josh was about to open it for his mother, a hand appeared on the other side of the door's glass pane. They heard the clicking sound of a deadbolt, and then the bold-lettered, black OPEN sign that hung in the door was quickly flipped to CLOSED, right in front of their eyes. The sign flipper quickly turned his back and walked away. Josh was so stunned he jerked his head, raised his eyebrows and looked toward his mom in disbelief. She nearly knocked him aside, then tapped on the wooden part of the door with her keys. Although several people on stools swiveled toward the door and looked at them, no one moved. They just sat there, chewing and staring like a field of grazing dairy cattle. Next Katie aggressively knocked on the glass with her knuckles. A staring standoff ensued. The smell of fried onions and bacon wafted through the air, further igniting Josh's appetite. Had he known the bacon and onions were smothering liver, his saliva might have stifled itself.

"Would someone let us IN," Katie said in her sternest commanding voice.

Suddenly the same man who had flipped the sign approached the door again. "Thank goodness," Josh whispered to his mom. Without a word, the man pointed to the hours posted in the picture window, then disappeared. Katie and Josh both looked at their wristwatches. It was 6:00 P.M., straight up, just when Harry's Grill closed.

"Welcome to Pardon ME Ville," Katie hissed rather than spoke. "Let's go. We'll check in real quick and find out where there's another place. Surely there's something." They got into the SUV in silence. As Katie backed out, looking behind her to merge into the stream of traffic, Josh watched the people at the counter swivel their stools back toward their plates. "Show's over," he mumbled.

"What?" Katie asked as she put it into gear.

"Nothing. Nothing, Mom. No wonder you have your own names for this place."

Katie drove around the square, veering off onto West Main Street. Within four blocks, she turned on her directional and pulled up in front of the Lamp Post. It was painted entirely in an unnatural shade of blue with a hand-made sign in the window that said UNDER NEW MANAGMENT.

"I'm not holding much hope out for computers, Mom. At least this guy obviously doesn't have a spell checker!" Again, Josh laughed at his own joke. Katie sighed, gave him a disgusted look, then opened her door and exited.

"Wait here," she said, then slammed the car door and strode with determination toward the entrance that had a hand-painted sign on it announcing RING BELL FOR SERV-ICE, to which she responded, after trying in vain to open the locked door. A young woman wearing a broad smile swiftly unlocked the door and said, "Welcome to the Lamp Post. You must be Ms. Durbin." Before Katie knew what had happened, the woman took Katie's right hand in her right hand and patted the top of it with her left. "I'm Jessica Joy. We hope to be a welcome night-light during your stay. We extend our sympathies upon the death of your aunt, ma'am, and are at your service."

Katie was stunned into inaction. She stood there one step down from the doorstep, mouth agape, staring into the sincere, soft hazel eyes of the long-haired brunette who was far from the old, dirty, crotchety person she'd expected.

"For goodness sakes, where are my manners?" Jessica said. She kept hold of Katie's hand while she led her into the little room that served as a lobby. Katie noticed, when Jessica finally let go of her hand, that she looked to be about six months pregnant behind her delicate muslin dress with blue and rose embroidered flowers around the neckline.

"How was your trip here, Ms. Durbin? You must be exhausted."

"Our trip was uneventful. And yes, I am a bit tired."

Jessica puckered up her heart-shaped mouth in a gesture of sympathy. "Well, we'll see if we can't get you settled in for the night. As you requested, I've reserved two of our deluxe rooms for you and . . ." she paused for a moment, then decided to just end her sentence with "you."

"One's for me and one's for my son, Joshua."

"Oh, I hope he's not just sitting in the car. Please invite him in."

"That's okay. He's actually quite hungry, and he's just waiting for me to reappear so we can find a place to eat. We were hoping you could help direct us."

Jessica immediately looked at her wristwatch. "Too late for Harry's."

"Yes, we found that out at exactly 6:00 P.M., when he locked us out trying to enter."

"Oh, I'm so sorry for that terrible greeting. Lester, Lester K. Biggs, is one of the nicest people you'll ever meet, and he has the biggest ol' heart. He's always got a jar out on his counter asking people to donate to whatever cause has moved him. He does have some rules that are unbendable, though, and closing time is one of them. After we get you settled in your rooms, I'll give you the name of a couple places that are close by."

Jessica moved herself behind the counter and retrieved two registration cards with Katie's name neatly written along the top line of each. "Would you like to see the rooms before you check in, Ms. Durbin?"

"No. You're the only motel in town anyway, aren't you?" Katie realized after she'd spoken this truth that she had wounded Jessica, as it showed all over her face.

"Yes, ma'am. We are. But Paul and me have worked real

hard to not take advantage of that. We don't want you to stay here unless you're happy, though. If you don't find us to your liking, the next closest one is the Ramada Inn near the mall in Hethrow, the next town over. We bought this place about eight months ago," she said, flipping the registration cards in her hands. "It was in a pretty sorry condition, but we've . . ." Her sentences were coming one right after the other in what was beginning to sound like a life's story.

"I'm sure it'll be just fine," Katie said with a tone of finality. Anything to move past this moment. "But why don't you show it to me first anyway." Katie sighed, her tone of voice relenting. She saw no cause to further humiliate someone who was obviously so fragile.

Jessica turned around and grabbed two of the keys from the twelve hooks behind her that were mounted on a piece of maple wood with scrollwork on the corners. "Follow me, Ms. Durbin." Together they walked in silence to room number eleven out of a total twelve. Jessica slipped the key into the lock and turned the knob. Katie took in the surprisingly welcome sight. The room, although somewhat crowded with two beds, was painted a very light lavender with a hand-stenciled border of green ivy. The bedspreads were a lavender-and-green floral pattern, and they flowed onto a light green carpet. Obviously a low-grade carpet, Katie thought, her Realtor's eye never at rest, but new and an excellent color with the rest of the decor.

"The bathroom is this way," Jessica said, even though it was obvious. She flipped on the light and motioned for Katie to come look. Again, it was small, but it had very pleasing colors and decorations.

Katie noticed the decorative basket on the counter containing Avon sample packets. Jessica saw Katie looking and said, "Oh, my friend sells Avon, and I thought some nice fragrances and bath samples would make it homey. I buy all my shampoo and such from her, and she always gives me a handful of samples for the rooms as long as I put her business card in the basket." Katie considered the bad business sense of someone who would give out samples to people who were only in town for a night.

"It's fine," Katie said in as warm a tone as she could muster.

"Would you like to see the other room, ma'am?"

"No, I trust it is just as nice."

"Why don't you just go ahead and take these keys. You can officially check in after dinner," Jessica said.

"No. Business first." Always, Katie thought, business first. As soon as the transaction was complete, Jessica gave Katie the names of three fairly nearby restaurants; two were chains, and the other was a smorgasbord. "Of course, there's always the snack bar at Wal-Mart just out of town," Jessica added. "I really do love their barbecue!" Katie muttered a stiff thank-you and went out to the car.

"Well?" Josh asked. "How's the rooms? And did you find a place for us to eat?"

Much to his surprise, his mother said the rooms were "quaint, clean, small but colorful." As for the food, although he didn't understand what she meant, he did understand food was soon to follow.

"Fasten your seat belt, Josh. We're heading for a culinary feast. I didn't know smorgasbords still existed. No doubt they'll have a tofu bar," she said sarcastically. And even he had to grin at that absurd possibility!

Alex my man! Yours truly checked into the Lamp Post motel in Pardon Me Ville (that's what mom calls it). Surprise surprise! I'm up and running, on-line and waiting to hear what's new in the neighborhood since I left town. Yeah, yeah. I know, it's only been a day since we talked, but HEY! You never know what blonde might appear on the scene. (Or brunette or redhead or purple-haired punker.) Of course I've got my eyes peeled here, although I'll probably have much better luck finding chickens rather than chicks.

Later Dude. Just wanted to let you know I'm available to the cosmos.

Joshmeister.

8

⸎⸎⸎

Arthur was sitting in his lopsided, fifteen-year-old La-Z-Boy watching TV when he saw The Tank coming up his driveway. "Oh, no. Not again!" he exclaimed to the universe.

"What? Did you say something, Arthur?" Jessie was in the kitchen slicing tomatoes she had purchased from Your Store earlier in the day. While she was busy slicing the mostly green, hard, tasteless things grown in someone's hothouse, she was daydreaming about the tomatoes they would get from their garden toward the end of summer. Fat. Blood red. Juice running down her arms as she ate them right off the vine like apples . . .

"I said, 'Oh, NO!'" Arthur bellowed. Jessie heard the leg support to the La-Z-Boy snap down at the same time she noticed the trail of dust coming up their driveway. She didn't need to ask what Arthur was talking about.

"Oh, I forgot to tell you that Dorothy said her door wasn't closing right and that she'd be coming by sometime this week."

"Glad you warned me," Arthur said as he strode up behind her to head out the door, but not before picking up a slice of tomato from the cutting board. He popped it in his mouth before she could say anything. "This tomato tastes as bad as The Tank looks," he said after two chews.

Jessie opened her mouth to respond but realized that, as odd as it might seem, this time Arthur was right. He spit out the partially chewed stuff into the garbage can near the back door, then marched across the yard toward The Tank, which had pulled up right inside his old shed turned garage turned shed. Although his face was kind of torqued up from the tomato, he was hoping Dorothy would take it as his silent commentary on The Tank's presence yet again.

The reality was, of course, quite different from what he always made it appear. Although he had long ago retired from fixing cars, that did not include The Tank. She was different. She was old, like him, and set in her ways. He was the only mechanic who'd ever worked on her, and he intended to keep things that way. Besides, today's sissy mechanics—and how they even dared call themselves mechanics he didn't know—only knew how to hook up electronic gizmos, which certainly wouldn't work on The Tank, nor would she take a liking to them. Why, there was no more to that, he used to say, than putting a thermometer in a baby's behind and thinking that would tell you what was really wrong with your child! No, The Tank needed careful consideration.

Sheba ran up to Arthur's legs, wagging her tail as fast as it would go. He gave her a head nod, which she accepted, then she ran off smelling the ground, scooting here and yonder.

Dorothy maneuvered herself out of the car door while trying to protect it from further damage in the familiarly tight quarters in the shed. She then slammed it the best she could, considering she only had about a foot and a half to work with. On cue and just as she suspected, the door didn't shut all the way. "Well," she finally said.

"Well," Arthur repeated.

"Well, I reckon, you know why I'm here, and if you don't, just take a gander at that," she said, pointing to the gap. "I've probably taken another year off the end of my life wearing myself out trying to get this door to shut right. And frankly, Arthur, I don't have that many years left!"

They traded places, and Arthur put the door through the same drill. Again, it didn't close right. Dorothy grinned like a satisfied ninny. Arthur looked at her and said, "Yup. Door doesn't close." They both just stood there looking at it for a spell until they were distracted by a chicken jutting by the door with Sheba close behind.

"Sheba! Get your naughty self over here right now!" Dorothy yelped. Sheba slunk into the shed and sat down beside Dorothy, putting her head against her leg in order to make up.

Arthur walked along the edge of the shed wall until he came to his giant rubber mallet. "It's all in the right tools," he said. Then he proceeded to bang around, first on the door above the window, then on the latch itself. Finally he tested his work and *voilà*! Slam it went, right the way it was supposed to.

"Had I known *that* was all it would take, I would have wound up and given her a few good licks myself! Probably would have helped my stress level."

"What have you got to be stressed about, Dorothy? Being on time for your next Hookers meeting?" He gave her a lopsided grin as he passed her by to hang his mallet back up.

"I imagine you'd be quite surprised to find out, Arthur. But today's not the day you're going to."

Just then Jessie appeared. "Do I have to worry about you two alone out here in the shed?" she teased.

"Not in the least," Arthur responded before Dorothy could open her mouth. "I can't get along with the one I got. Why would I make eyes at another one?"

"And don't you forget it, buster!" Jessie retorted.

"How's it going, Dorothy?" Jessie asked while rubbing her hands on her slacks. "You look tired. Everything okay?"

Dorothy sighed, picked up Sheba, gave her a few solid strokes, as though centering herself, sighed again, opened her mouth to speak, then shut it. Jessie cocked her head, but she didn't speak either. Finally Dorothy uttered, "Fine. Tired, but fine."

"Everything okay?"

"Maybe."

"Anything we can help with?"

"Nope. Just me and the Lord and a few folks in between are workin' on this one."

"Keep us posted, friend," Jessie said. "If there's anything, anything you need us for, you know we're right here."

Dorothy picked up Sheba and pointed to the rear open window of The Tank. The dog leapt out of her arms and into the backseat.

"Thanks for caring, Jessie. I imagine you'll all find out soon enough, should the Lord surprise even me." She gently opened the door and sneaked inside, having to turn somewhat sideways, the same way she had exited. Then she cranked the engine and put it in reverse.

"Look out, chickens!" Arthur hollered. "Dorothy's in reverse!" Jessie elbowed him a good one. With that, Dorothy gunned out of the shed, toppling Sheba in the process, then down the driveway they went.

"What do you make of that, Arthur?"

"I'd say she purrs like a kitten."

Jessie was about ready to give him another good elbow to the rib when it suddenly dawned on her that although she was wondering about Dorothy's peculiar behavior, he was talking about The Tank.

9

Sharon Teller sat in a deep, expensive-looking, brown, buttery-leather chair in the reception area at Craig & Craig Developers. She was waiting to meet with Colton Craig, the senior partner in his real estate monster of a machine. At least that's the way she personally looked at it. From a professional point of view as a reporter representing the *Partonville Press*, she knew she had to wear a neutral hat during the interview and writing, but it wasn't going to be easy. She detested everything about his so-called progress. All she had seen it accomplish so far was more traffic and more homes, less land, less privacy, less of everything she loved. The town of Hethrow, to the east, where most of the growth had occurred, felt like it had slithered up in the night and was poised like a python, mouth agape, ready to swallow Partonville alive, and each Craig brother was an eyeball.

She flicked a *New York Times* in front of her face in an attempt to act as if she were reading when in reality she was inner-dialoguing, mustering all the mental capabilities she could in order to live up to the press credentials she carried in her pocket. Just before she feared her head would explode from concentration and constraint, the receptionist's buzzer startled her so badly that a strange little squeaky noise escaped from her throat. *Oh, now* there's *professionalism!*

"Mr. Craig will see you now, Ms. Teller. Go through this door, and his office will be the last on your left." Without swiveling her chair, the receptionist pointed a finger over her own shoulder toward the door behind her.

"Thank you." Sharon walked past the receptionist and swung open the heavy oak door that had tiny pieces of beveled glass spelling out the name CRAIG set in the middle of what looked to be a lead glass panel. The overt decadence prickled her hide. She fingered her press card like a touchstone to keep her mental game on course. Down the long hall she walked, noticing that every door was closed. The faint smell of burning cigar wafted out from somewhere, and she hoped it wasn't from within the office she was about to enter. She stood in front of the door for a moment, took a deep breath, then knocked.

"Come in, Ms. Teller," a firm voice from behind the door announced. She snapped her head erect, threw her shoulders back and walked with determination into the office.

She was stunned at the sight before her. Colton Craig's office was nearly as big as her entire little Partonville home! He had a corner office, and both exterior walls were, from nearly floor to ceiling, glass with a slight tint of gray. He overlooked what used to be a quiet little town called Hethrow but what now, in her opinion, more closely resembled a yucky Baby Chicago. Of course, she had to admit she was personally familiar with every mall and strip mall in the entire vicinity, being the clotheshorse she was. She also enjoyed the vast selection of salons to choose from, and attending some of the new junior college's cultural events, and . . . yes, she did have those conflicts.

The room itself was austere. Nothing extra. No piles of

papers, blueprints or building models were visible. His gigantic desk had such large claw-foot legs on it that it looked like it might begin to lumber to life at any moment. It was set on the diagonal facing the windows, and his back was to her. *Pretty trusting for someone who makes so many enemies,* she thought. When she was closing the door behind her, he swiveled in his chair and said, "Leave it open, please. And welcome."

She strode across the room with steps of authority, hand extended in front of her, swallowing hard just before making contact. He had the deepest green eyes she'd ever seen and was very tan for spring, accentuating his whiter-than-white teeth. His hand was large, and the shake warm and firm. She was thrown slightly off base by his staggering good looks and feared she was blushing at her own feminine vulnerabilities.

"I'm Colton Craig, but please call me Colton," he said.

"Sharon Teller." Her voice sounded like that of a twelve-year-old rather than a twenty-five-year-old professional woman. *Get a grip!*

"Please, sit down," he said as he pointed to the over-stuffed burgundy leather couch directly in front of his desk. She noticed that the *Partonville Press* lay open in front of him. It was the only thing on the highly polished mahogany aside from his phone and an autographed baseball in a glass box.

She quickly got herself arranged, whipping out her notebook from her large handbag that also served as a briefcase. She rested it on her lap, then removed a tape recorder before setting her bag on the forest green carpet. *Looks like the color of money to me.* Before she set the tape recorder on the desk she looked up at him and asked, "Is it okay if I tape our conversation, Mr. Craig?" She was not going to take him up on his first-name-basis offer, and he raised an eyebrow at that but let it pass without acknowledgment.

"Of course. I have nothing to keep off the record, and I love being quoted verbatim. Not that I think you'd get things wrong. You're quite an excellent reporter, Ms. Teller," he said as he tapped the paper with the back of his right-hand index knuckle. "Lively writing. Passionate." There was something about the way he said "passionate."

She suddenly felt like a deer in the crosshairs of a marksman. She fumbled with the tape recorder and finally got it in place on the front of his desk, microphone facing him. By the time she'd opened her steno and taken the lid off her pen, she had collected herself, mentally pulling her own six-shooter out of its holster. She pushed the "record" button. *Fire round one!*

"Mr. Craig, word around Partonville is that your firm is seeking a land deal to the east of Partonville proper. Thus far we've been unable to verify the rumors. I'm here to collect the facts from the horse's mouth so we can either help put a stop to the rumors or substantiate them."

"Well, the horse's mouth," and he paused just a fraction of a second here, which was long enough for the left corner of his lip to curl, "says it's true that Craig & Craig Developers is always open to expand our progressive development. We believe progress and growth are good things."

"Are you talking to any Partonville farmers, Mr. Craig?"

He grinned a total teeth-showing grin and again paused for a moment, tilting his head forward toward her, as if to ricochet the answer to her via silence. After studying her blank face for a moment, he then proceeded.

"If . . ."—dramatic pause, more teeth—"if we were, Ms.

Teller, we certainly wouldn't be talking about it. And please don't read more into that answer than I've stated. I'm sure an esteemed reporter such as you understands the sensitivity of the real estate world well enough to know the drill. I do like your tenacity, though."

Truth be known, she didn't know the drill. This was her first venture into real estate waters, and she was mad at herself for being caught in her own ignorance. She was sure as shootin' gonna research it when she got back to the office! *What the heck was Harold thinking, sending me out to embarrass myself like this? He should have come himself!* Colton Craig was obviously reading her like a short book.

"So in other words . . ." she said, trying to buy herself a little time while nearly breaking a sweat trying to reveal nothing in her eyes, even though she knew it was too late.

"No, I thought we were recording my words exactly," he said, intruding into her sentence.

"Of course we are," she said politely. "But just to clarify your intentions . . ."

"Make that our *vision,* please. Just to clarify our vision," he said, again intruding into her sentence with his silky voice.

"So, your *vision* is to build a housing development where?" Her voice lifted at the end of the question.

"Our vision is to continue seeking possibilities, Ms. Teller, wherever they might present themselves. As you know, Hethrow has undergone a complete face-lift and growth spurt since our firm began development when Ford Motors announced they were bringing a plant to town a decade ago. Not only have we created more housing, but downtown businesses have flourished and grown, the new junior college is drawing from several counties, an upscale mall was established and, as a result of all that, more jobs are available, breathing further life into the community and economy. We believe we've helped improve the integrity of the entire area."

Simultaneously she noticed the dark ring around his irises and bristled at the use of the word *integrity. As though you have a clue what it means! More and more of everything including more money in your pockets doesn't automatically add up to integrity in anyone's stretch of the imagination. Although Partonville might be lacking in a few things, it certainly isn't lacking integrity! Why, it is oozing with integrity, from businesses to producing farms, WE ARE OOZING INTEGRITY!*

She sat there watching the tape recorder run for a moment while she leashed her emotions lest they come bursting out of her lips.

"Do you have any questions, Ms. Teller? Do you disagree with what I've said? Am I boring you?"

"I do wonder at your use of the word *integrity,* sir." *Oops.*

"You question my integrity, Ms. Teller? In what way?"

"Not *your* integrity, just your use of the word, as though more of everything equals integrity. I guess it's a matter of semantics," she said, working to bail herself out of saying what she'd already said and what she really meant.

"Yes. Semantics." For the first time since their eyeballing of one another, Colton looked a tad bristled himself.

Sharon leaned forward, shut off her tape recorder and dropped it into her bag. She folded her spiral steno so the cover was protecting the pages, ran her pen down through the spiral, catching the clip over the edge to keep it where it belonged—she had to have control over *something*—and stood up. All this without making eye contact with Mr. Craig, who, she knew, was studying her closer than she'd like to be studied at the moment.

"I thank you for your time." She pulled out a business card and tossed it on his desk. "I'd like to keep our readers abreast of any events concerning this. Please give me a call should there be any solid developments."

"I assume this means our time together is over for now, Ms. Teller?"

I will not let him pull my chain! She flung her bag over her shoulder and stretched out her hand to shake good-bye. "Yes, sir. There is no need to keep talking about nothing. When and if there is something, we'll try again."

The warmth of his parting handshake stayed with her all the way to her car.

Sharon sat in her Chevy in the Craig & Craig parking lot, reflecting on her mix of emotions. She was angry, for sure. The man was arrogant. For sure. He also had the widest shoulders she'd seen for some time and . . . *STOP IT! Go get yourself some lunch and GET A GRIP!*

Driving down the main drag, she craned her neck from side to side, taking stock of restaurants and waffling with herself and her taste buds about whether to have Mexican food, a sub sandwich, chicken or . . . *I can have whatever I want. Whatever I have a taste for, I can find it here!* As she passed by Hethrow General Hospital, she recalled reading about their new trauma unit and cutting-edge birthing fa-cilities in one of the *Daily Courier's* editions. Of course, she usually read the syndicated paper in order to . . . um . . . keep abreast of what was happening in the world. The world, not just Partonville. The world, with ethnic diversity and research and political challenges and maybe a husband on the horizon, since Partonville seemed to nearly be fresh out of bachelors. . . .

Craig had talked about more jobs. Many of Partonville's youth had for some time been fleeing after high school to pursue higher education. More often than not, they didn't seem to be returning. Job opportunities were elsewhere. *Would it be a* bad *thing to have more jobs come to Partonville? How much more debt-free from college loans might* I *be if the junior college in Hethrow had been in place when* I *went off to college?*

Sharon snapped to attention and slammed her brakes on just in time to keep from rear-ending the car in front of her. About the twelfth car back from the red light. The red light causing a yet unknown traffic backup in quiet little Partonville. Where things weren't so crowded. Partonville, where everybody knew her name and her family. Her roots. Her life.

10

Tess Walker's funeral would take place early in the morning, and final arrangements needed to be made. Dorothy was in need of a distraction from her own thoughts and was happy to have a task at the church, especially since Nellie Ruth would be assisting. Nellie Ruth was usually humming while she worked, and since music had always been a balm to Dorothy when she was troubled, her friend's company brought many gifts.

Nellie Ruth loved being on the altar guild at United Methodist for several reasons, not the least of which was that it gave her a chance to spend more time with Dorothy. It also allowed her to spend time in this place of deep personal meaning and spiritual transformation.

Nellie Ruth had been raised in St. Louis, Missouri, where she'd learned too much about dark things at a very early age. From the time she was nine years old, her father had violated and abused her in unspeakable ways in their small apartment. When she was sixteen, her mom died of a heart ailment. Caring for her alcoholic father and putting food on the table became her lot in life. She had no worldly experiences other than the torment within her home and a job she held for three years at a local grocery. She did everything from mopping to restocking shelves to checking out customers' orders. She was happy to have a reason to be out of the house and did enjoy her job, aside from the fact that she didn't believe it would ever earn her enough to be able to strike out on her own.

She "escaped" that life when her father died. He was struck by a car in front of the tavern when he stumbled off the curb in front of the vehicle. Nellie Ruth was just eighteen years old. Without thinking things through, the red-haired girl with the oval face and sad eyes packed a suitcase, took her last two weeks' pay, filled the gas tank of the Ford and headed north until she stopped crying. It happened that was in Partonville.

Dorothy had come to town to set up the altar for Sunday's service that day when she discovered this skinny young woman sleeping in her car in the church parking lot. When she knocked on the window, it startled Nellie Ruth so badly that she awakened and began crying all over again.

Dorothy asked if she was okay, but Nellie Ruth couldn't even respond, she was heaving and sobbing so violently. Dorothy flatly stated that she wasn't leaving until Nellie Ruth came into the church, calmed down and assured her she was all right. She stood outside Nellie Ruth's locked driver's door in the pouring rain, hand on the door handle, silently praying, for nearly forty minutes.

Finally Nellie Ruth realized this woman meant what she said. She was too weak to drive a lick farther anyway. At last she dragged herself out of the car, and Dorothy led her into the church. There Nellie Ruth poured her heart out to this kind and gentle woman who held her until she had spent all her emotions. Dorothy brought her a cup of hot tea after phoning May Belle to come set up the altar for her.

Dorothy's only explanation to May Belle was that she had an important mission. May Belle knew enough about Dorothy to believe it.

When Nellie Ruth was done with her cup of tea, Dorothy invited her back to the farm, telling her she could stay in the extra bedroom until she found a job and a place of her own. For reasons unknown even to herself, that's just what Nellie Ruth did.

After three days of nothing but sleeping and eating and allowing Dorothy to nurse her back to life, Nellie Ruth was ready to face the world. Dorothy got her a job at Your Store; she was a perfect fit and a great asset. Within three weeks, thanks to Dorothy and her husband's gracious ministering, hospitality and what could be described as nothing short of the healing powers of the land on Crooked Creek Farm, she had saved enough to pay a month's advance rent at a rooming house in town and had become strong enough to tackle independence. She went on to become a head checker, a produce manager and now was assistant manager of the entire store. As in the days of her youth, she still loved working in the grocery business. She enjoyed everything about it, from the bustle of the people to the fragrance of freshly ground coffee to the orderly shelves. But especially she loved silently praying for unsuspecting people buying everything from fresh oranges to baby food to thumbtacks.

Now here these two women stood, side by side, discussing preparations for the sanctuary for Tess Walker's wake and funeral. A couple of floral arrangements had already arrived, including Katie's, whose stock sympathy card read

"Kathryn and Joshua." The altar needed to be set up according to Pastor Delbert's wishes. Back pews must be roped off so those attending would sit together. They didn't anticipate a very large crowd, and they were afraid people would scatter themselves around, making their numbers appear even smaller than they would be.

In the midst of their discussions, in walked Katie and Josh.

Before leaving Chicago, Katie had made arrangements to meet Thursday morning at nine-thirty with "please-call-me-Pastor-Delbert," as she referred to him when speaking to Josh about their appointment. Pastor Delbert Carol, Jr., had corrected her three times during their phone conversations with exactly those words after she called him Father Carol, not knowing his proper title. At 9:30 A.M. sharp, Katie walked into the sanctuary to find two women she didn't know talking about her Aunt Tess's arrangements as though they were in charge.

When Dorothy looked up and saw Katie and Josh standing there, she didn't say a word but headed right toward them with her arms outstretched. Since Katie didn't expect such an old lady to move so quickly, before she knew what had hit her, Dorothy threw her arms around her and embraced her solidly to her chest. "Why, Katie Durbin! I haven't seen you since you were a tyke, but I'd recognize you anywhere!" Her determined hug and solid back patting continued. "I'm sorry this is what's finally bringing us together after all these years. Oh, how I loved spending time with your mother and aunt when we were growing up!" Dorothy finally released Katie and backed off a bit to look at the stunned woman's face.

"Oh, honey! I didn't mean to squeeze the life out of you!" she said, patting Katie on her left shoulder with her right hand.

"And you would be?" Katie looked from Dorothy to Nellie Ruth, who had walked up behind Dorothy, then back again into Dorothy's face.

"Forgive me, child. I'm Dorothy Wetstra. Like wet straw but without the end *w*. I'm on the altar guild here at United Methodist. I was born and raised and will undoubtedly die right here in Partonville, so I reckon I know just about everybody." She noticed Katie was now looking over her shoulder, so she turned around and said, "And this here is Nellie Ruth. Nellie Ruth McGregor. She's on the altar guild too. We've been talking about your aunt's arrangements. We're so sorry about your loss, honey."

Katie hadn't been called honey by anyone since her mom had died. Although it did stir something warm within her, she also found it disturbing, considering this woman didn't really know her from a river of caffe latte.

"And who is this?" Dorothy asked, pointing and moving toward Josh, who was grinning like a hyena at his mother's obvious discomfort with the situation.

"Josh," he answered, extending his hand to ward off any possible hug attack.

"This is my son, Joshua Kinney."

"I'm sorry for your loss, too, honey," Dorothy said. Nellie Ruth hadn't opened her mouth yet; she had long ago learned that Dorothy knew how to handle strangers.

"Oh, that's okay," Josh replied almost happily. "I didn't know her anyway." Katie turned on her heels and threw Josh one of her looks that implied pending disaster should he not be more careful with his words.

"Now, can we get you a drink of coffee or water or something? You must be tired after all that driving. What on earth time did you leave this morning to get here so early?"

"We came in last night," Josh replied before his mom could open her mouth. "We stayed at the Lamp Post."

"Oh, that lovely young Jessica Joy and her husband Paul have been working so hard, adding so many nice personal touches to the place. When I come into town I see her out there in the early morning tending to those flowers, and after dinner I see him carrying a ladder or a bucket of paint from one place to another and her tagging along, hands full of whatever. Heavens, he's already put in a full day's work in the mines and her carrying that little one around inside her now. How was everything? I'm sure it was lovely. And if I'd known you were going to be in town I would have invited you out to the farm for supper. My goodness me, it's not bad enough your having to lose a relative but then to be in town with no one to talk to!"

"Actually it worked out just fine. We were tired and probably wouldn't have been good company anyway," Katie said, wondering at a woman who would invite people she didn't *really* know to have dinner in her home.

"What time did you arrive?" Nellie Ruth asked, having realized she didn't want her silence to be construed as indifference.

"About six o'clock," Josh answered, enjoying the friendliness of these two ladies.

"So you *were* here for supper then?" Dorothy asked.

Katie just nodded an affirmative.

"Did you dine at Harry's?"

"Nope. He pretty much locked us out before we could get in," Josh said, taking great delight in telling the details of the story, keeping them engaged in more conversation than he knew his mother would invite.

"Oh, my!" Dorothy remarked. "He is set in his ways. A good man but pretty unbending, I'm afraid."

"So we were told by Jessica. So we noticed ourselves," Katie said, revealing a little more edge to her voice than she would have liked.

Dorothy studied her for a moment, as though looking deep within her. It became a look so penetrating that it made Katie back up a step. Katie then inquired where she might find Pastor Delbert.

"Why, I imagine he's in his office, dear. Follow me." She was off and stepping before the phrase was out of her mouth. Nellie Ruth motioned for Katie and Josh to go ahead and told them she was going to stay and continue working. "I imagine I'll be seeing you shortly anyway," she said. "I'm sure Pastor Delbert will want to make sure we're all on the same page as he goes over things with you."

Katie and Josh followed Dorothy to the back of the sanctuary, the same way they'd come in, and then they made a right-hand turn toward a doorway at the end of the narthex. Katie fully expected to see an office when Dorothy opened the door and disappeared down a stairway. She turned around and looked at Josh, who shrugged his shoulders, then they both followed this speeding bullet of a woman. Dorothy hollered over her shoulder that the fellowship room was also "down here along with the Sunday school room, nursery and our adult Sunday school meeting place. Pastor Delbert's office is in the very back corner. He claims that since he came to us eleven years ago, following the death of his father, who had been our pastor for thirty-eight years, that he needed to have his own space and identity rather than moving into his father's office upstairs. We figure he could do whatever he wanted since he was the pastor. We long ago converted Pastor Delbert Senior's office into our library. Feel free to take a look around in there before you leave. In fact, I'll take you right to it when we're done with arrangements."

Katie listened, wrote off any need to visit a church library and considered how unusual it must be for a church to have pastors from the same family, especially ones who obviously stay around until they die. By the end of her thought they were entering Pastor's office.

Pastor Delbert Junior simultaneously stood and pushed back out of his chair, which shot like a bullet out from under him and rolled with such force that it crashed into the wall. It looked as if this chair launching was a common occurrence, as the wall behind him was dented and full of black marks. In fact, he appeared disheveled himself. His thinning hair was askew, and his glasses were slightly cockeyed. His medium stature was relaxed into bad posture. When he looked as if he might come around his desk, Katie quickly extended her hand. First surprised by Jessica's handhold, then taken off guard by Dorothy's hug, she wasn't about to let another show of affection blindside her again.

"You must be Katie Durbin. Welcome to United Methodist Church of Partonville. I'm sorry you're visiting us under such sad circumstances," Pastor said.

"Thank you. I appreciate all your help over the last few days. I can't imagine getting all the arrangements made without it." And she meant that with all that was within her. Dorothy quickly interjected something about turning this part over to them, then disappeared out of the room and back up the stairs.

"I'm happy to be of assistance. I just wish I could have known your aunt. Since I grew up in Partonville and my dad was the pastor here at United Methodist for so many years, I did get at least familiar with most of the names if not the people themselves. I knew where your aunt lived and that she had a sister in Chicago, but that was about it, I'm sorry to say. As I recall, my dad used to call on your Aunt Tess quite often when I was young, although I don't believe she actually ever attended our church. I'm not quite sure why he was so rigorous in his visits, but I do know Dad wasn't one to give up on what he considered might be a lost sheep. I understand she kept pretty much to herself these last many years."

"I wouldn't know about that, Pastor Delbert. I hadn't seen her myself for over ten years. We only corresponded once a year, and that was Christmas cards with maybe a line or two in them. She was a bit unusual." Katie figured she'd take the high road and leave it at that.

"Yes. Well, just the same, God knew her, and we're here for you now. We'd like to help you see to it that she has a good Christian sendoff. I've been talking to Eugene Casey down at Casey's, and he'll be sending your aunt's cremated remains over about two-thirty this afternoon, in time for this evening's visitation, even though you've made it clear we're not displaying the urn. It seems as though everything is pretty much in place for her next journey."

You make it sound like crazy Aunt Tess will be arriving for a bon voyage party! How can people involved in the church sound so cheery about death and so sad about people they don't know?

"There is no urn," she said flatly.

"No urn?"

"No. Mr. Casey described a few of them to me on the

phone, but I didn't see the point in having one, since I'll be disposing of her ashes anyway." She realized that sounded a bit harsh, and it was reflected on Pastor's face. But then facts were facts. She hadn't even kept her mother's ashes. Although the loss of her loving mom had deeply pierced her heart, she knew keeping that silver urn would neither help heal the wound nor give her comfort. In fact, it might even induce self-pity when she looked at it, and pity of any type wasn't acceptable.

Although Katie and her mom hadn't always seen eye to eye, they were quite close. After all, until Katie married it had pretty much been the two of them against the world, even considering the differences in their country girl heart vs. city slicker head approaches to life. Truthfully, why Clarice had ever moved that obvious country girl heart to the city to begin with was a mystery that had always puzzled Katie and died with her mom. When Aunt Tess inquired at Clarice's funeral whether Katie was going to keep or spread her mother's ashes, Katie simply asked her aunt if she'd like them, believing Partonville was where her mom belonged anyway. Aunt Tess became teary-eyed at Katie's offer, then quietly accepted the urn.

And now, no, there would be no urn for Aunt Tess.

"Please, won't you be seated." Pastor pulled up an avocado green, circa seventies chair with a frayed cushion, then retrieved the beige metal folding chair propped against his office wall. He seated himself behind his desk. Josh stepped behind the cushioned chair to push it up for his mom. She took one look at the stained and ragged fabric, another at her silk slacks, then told Josh he could have "the comfortable seat."

"All righty then, let's go over the final details," Pastor

said as Katie seated herself on the edge of the folding chair. "Dorothy and Nellie Ruth are figuring the layout for the flowers. And by the way, I hope you noticed your flowers did arrive. They're lovely. The ladies will also be tending to some of the details in the sanctuary so that we can be intimately gathered for the service. Gertrude Hands has agreed to come play the organ for us while people are filtering in and after the service."

"What else do we have to decide?" Katie asked.

"I realize you hadn't seen your aunt recently, but do you know if she had any favorite hymns or Bible verses? Or might there be any stories, funny or poignant, or things you did know about your aunt you'd like us to share?"

Katie was at a total loss. She sat staring at him, unblinking, for a moment, then realized she had nothing with which to respond. *Think. Think, Katie! Surely there's some bit of information you can share.* Try as she might, however, nothing came to mind other than her own annoyance with her aunt's peculiarities.

She tried to recall a story her mother might have shared about her sister. Again, all she could come up with was her own words, words that visibly stung her mother: "Mom, I just don't have time right now to hear about your crazy sister!" How many times had Katie brushed off her mom the last year of her life as she tried to share her concerns for her only sister? Fretted about what would happen to her after she was gone? Her mother, being a gentle soul, had never even chastised Katie. Just sighed. Yes, she remembered her mother sighing, rubbing Katie gently on the shoulder, then softly suggesting that Katie perhaps needed to get more rest.

Katie began to feel somewhat nauseated. Detached. Alone.

She realized that she had no one to call, no family to seek, no memories to mine in which to find answers to what should be an easy question. Only her responses to life, which suddenly felt like icy cold smacks to her own face.

No stories. Katie had no stories of her aunt, whose existence she'd spent more than a decade trying to deny and whom her mother had spent a lifetime loving—just as she'd loved Katie. Katie had actively refused to embrace this entire Partonville part of her mother's past, this small-town background. After all, SHE WAS A CITY GIRL! She had been filled with nothing but such distaste for this place . . . so put out with the task . . .

She became overwhelmed by the fact that her last tie to her mother was now gone, and she had never done one thing to maintain it. She was blindsided by a barrage of reality, or repressed grief, or deep sorrow, or something she couldn't name. She only knew one thing: she missed her mother, and now her last link to the woman who had borne her was gone.

Her chest became tight, and drawing a deep breath seemed necessary but impossible. She deliberately and loudly inhaled and exhaled. Her heart began racing, and her hands felt clammy. She actually thought for a moment that she might faint or become physically ill, and she turned white as a sheet. Although up to now she'd been perched with perfect posture on the edge of the folding chair, she leaned back in an attempt to ground herself.

"Mom! Are you all right?" Josh asked, rising from his chair.

Pastor's chair thunked against the wall as he launched himself. "Katie? Do you need a glass of water?" He had moved beside her and was patting her hand. She could do nothing but allow him to do so and in fact welcomed the touch of reality since her equilibrium was still swimming.

"Will you please run upstairs, Josh, and have Dorothy bring us a glass of water?"

"Sure. Just make sure she doesn't fall out of the chair, okay?" Although Josh headed toward the door he didn't leave the room until Katie spoke.

"Yes, Josh. A glass of water would be nice. I'm okay. Go ahead and find me one, please."

Josh hiked the stairs two at a time and ran into the sanctuary. Dorothy saw him bound halfway up the aisle. She was in the back corner tying off the last pew, and he didn't see her. Ran right past her. Nellie Ruth was nowhere in sight.

"Is everything okay, Josh?" Dorothy asked, nearly scaring him out of his wits.

"Mom needs a drink of water right away. She's a little dizzy or something." He wore a look of panic on his face.

"Oh, my! I'll be right there. Go ahead on back downstairs and tell them I'm on my way." Immediately she scurried to the tiny room off the library that served as a makeshift kitchen and hospitality room for Sunday morning coffee and rolls. She grabbed a plastic glass and a paper towel, ran the cold water until it actually ran cold, filled up the glass, soaked the paper towel and sped down the stairs. When she arrived, Pastor was still standing next to Katie holding her hand, and Josh stood next to Pastor. He couldn't remember his mother ever looking this vulnerable or weak, and it was scaring him.

"Here we go, honey," Dorothy said. She took Katie's left hand, the one Pastor wasn't stroking, and wrapped Katie's fingers around the glass and waited until she took a sip, then she went around behind her and held the paper towel to Katie's forehead, gently coaxing her to lean back and relax.

Katie still felt a bit light-headed . . . and there was something about Dorothy's soothing voice and the way Pastor was holding her hand that miraculously allowed her simply to be still and receive what they were giving. She downed the entire glass of water and just sat there. One of Dorothy's hands was on her forehead and the other on her shoulder. Pastor was looking up into her face as he now kneeled in front of her trying to make eye contact. Josh looked over Pastor's shoulder with tender concern. She was cocooned in care, and she could do nothing but close her eyes and be in the moment, too weak to resist.

From the depths of her, she felt a stirring. A mild stinging sensation infiltrated her nose and eyes, and tears begin to pool beneath her eyelids. She scrunched her eyelids hard together, but it was no use. Tears began to stream over her lower lids, down her cheeks, around the curve of her chin, down her neck. A quiet sob manifested in her throat and made itself known to those around her in a quick inhale and exhale.

She became aware of Dorothy's hands, now gently rubbing forward and back across the top of her shoulders, the moist paper towel having been dropped to the floor. Pastor continued to kneel and now had his eyes closed, praying, cradling both of Katie's hands in his.

Josh leaned his hips back against the desk, feeling somewhat weak himself. For the first time in his life, he saw his mother, outwardly and without holding back, begin to cry.

Katie Mabel Carol Durbin had, unbeknownst to her, in the basement of the United Methodist Church of Partonville, surrounded by those who genuinely cared and in a moment of God's grace, come home to herself. For the first time, she full-out grieved for the loss of her mother—her ballast, the one person who had loved her unconditionally, no matter how impossible she'd been.

11

"**P**ass me the sugar, will ya, Sharon?" Today's Wednesday edition of the *Partonville Press* sprawled in front of him on the counter at Harry's, Harold, the editor, red pencil in hand, was engaged in his usual routine of reading the paper from page one through the last period on the last page, ads and all. The only time he missed doing so was two years ago March, the day his daughter delivered his first grandchild. Rather than spend time on his own creation, he had examined and cuddled one of the best creations God ever plunked into his arms. His rating system for papers was how many red circles he drew, the fewer the better. Baby Carolyn got a zero-circle rating, only one he'd ever given.

Sharon passed him the sugar, watched him pour in about three teaspoons full—no stirring; always said he liked discovering the sweet spot in the bottom—then sat quietly beside him while he finished the last two pages. She knew better than to try to engage his attention until the paper was closed. She twiddled with the button on the bottom of her cardigan, then twirled the hair behind her left ear, chewed on two of her fingernails and began twisting a paper napkin. Finally, Harold folded the paper, tucked it on the stool under him, swiveled to face her and said, "Two-circle day. Okay, Sharon. What'd ya get from the Craigs' office? From your gyrations the last few minutes, I'd say either nothing or enough to fill the entire paper."

Sharon broke eye contact, swiveled toward the counter and said, to the salt and pepper, "You should have gone yourself. I can't *believe* you sent me into the lion's den so unprepared. I'm just too green for this job. You should have known better, Mr. Crabb!" By this time her eyes welled up, her nose turned red and she'd ripped the paper napkin plumb in two.

"Whoa! Whoa, girlie girl! You are the best reporter whose byline I've had the privilege to run in my papers. You have good instincts, good control and a good head on your shoulders." Sharon's entire face and neck turned a bright red, same as they did every time Mr. Crabb complimented her. "What in the world has thrown you so off base?"

"Real estate," she said, dabbing each eye with each hand holding a half of napkin, black mascara circles appearing beneath her lower lids. "I just haven't been involved in big business real estate like this, and I'm afraid I was way out of my league. You should have educated me as to how things are done. And as for Colton Craig, that arrogant, self-righteous snob, well, he caught me right up in his web of . . . of . . . ARROGANCE and made me look like a fool!"

Harold stifled a smile. He'd met the Craig brothers at a convention once, and it didn't take much looking to realize that Colton Craig was obviously a well-seasoned, good-looking ladies' man. He'd impressed Harold—who wasn't easily impressed—with his charismatic presence and smooth talking. He suspected that Sharon, who was beet red again just talking about him, had responded just as his wife and every other woman in the place had: near drooling. Now, not that he didn't fully trust Martha, knowing positively well she was a devoted wife, mom and grandmother, but being seasoned all his life as a reporter and therefore an observer, he also understood the balance of human nature.

"Here," he said, sliding Sharon's own glass into her downward sight line, leaving a trail of water across the counter. "Take a sip of water, blow your nose and tell me what happened. From the beginning." Although Lester never approached them, Harold was sure he was all ears. Earl was sitting across the U from them slurping a soda, but certainly Earl wasn't a gossip—at least not a knowing one. Good thing the place wasn't loaded, Harold thought; that's why he usually picked two-thirty for his read-through, since lunchers were gone and the evening group hadn't arrived yet.

Sharon downed a few gulps, blew her nose on one half of the napkin, wadded it up with the other and clasped it in her hands. "Well, Mr. Crabb, first off, he has the most bragging type of office! I mean, have you ever *seen* Craig & Craig's offices?"

"No, although I've met the brothers Craig, I can't say as I've been in their offices. I will say that we surely shouldn't be judging a book by its cover, though, and—" Before he could end his sentence, she jumped right in.

"His office was nearly bigger than my entire home, and it overlooks Hethrow. I looked out that window and remembered when I used to ride Molly through that beautiful countryside, and now it's one parking lot and building after another, and I just couldn't stand to think that Partonville could become a mall one day and—"

Now it was Harold's turn to jump in. "Sharon, is that what he told you? He's planning on making Partonville a mall?"

"I don't know what he's planning, but you can bet it's something. Something to make him a fatter cat at our expense."

Harold grabbed her shoulders and swiveled her to face him. "Sharon Teller, I've never known you to be so judgmental. Not good for a reporter. When you say you don't know what he's planning, did you ask? And what was his response."

"Mostly he humiliated me, realizing I had no idea how the real estate game was played. He said, of course, that he was always looking for opportunities and, of course, I understood that should there be any talk, which he didn't confirm, that it wouldn't be public knowledge up front."

"Yes."

"Yes? You mean, *of course,* you knew all this, right?"

"Right."

"THEN WHY DIDN'T YOU TELL ME I'd look dumb asking him?"

"It never hurts to let someone know we're watching, no matter what either side reveals or doesn't. And now he knows the *Partonville Press* is on full alert to his dealings, and that's a good thing."

"Gads! Has everyone turned into Martha Stewart? That's what *he* said about development!"

"What's that?"

"That it's a good thing."

"And you think it isn't?"

"And you think it is?"

"Sharon, we seem to be caught in a loop here. Let's start over. First off, we are reporters who report the news, and no matter what we think or feel or believe, we're only supposed to be gathering and reporting the facts. Did you find out any new facts?"

"No. Only that I don't know anything about real estate deals."

"Okay, then, we have no story for now. Off the record and out of curiosity," Harold said, leaning in toward Sharon, "what are your personal opinions about development? And do you believe they represent everyone's opinion in Partonville?"

"Yes. No. Well, maybe. Honestly, I'm realizing I'm not even sure what *I* think about all of it. I mean, I was born and raised in Partonville. Although my daddy wasn't a farmer, since he worked in the mines all his life, most of our friends were and continue to be. I worry about those folks if land starts to disappear. Then again, they'd probably be set for life if they sold off. I hate traffic. I wonder what will happen to *all* of us if we turn into the next Hethrow. How will the entire country survive if we keep selling farmland? See what I mean? I'm confused! And still . . . I find myself traveling to Hethrow more and more often! Am *I* a sign of the times? Am *I* the next itchy generation?"

"You ask good, sensitive questions, Sharon. That's what makes you such a fine reporter. You know, some folks are going to be stuck in their ways no matter what. Any talk of change causes them to buck and kick. Some, well, farming's the only thing they know. Some of the younger folks, they just silently move on, or away. But one thing is for sure: ready or not, one day change *will* come."

"And which side of the fence do you sit on, Mr. Crabb?"

"Ever since Ford Motors arrived in Hethrow, I've been giving this whole topic a great deal of personal thought.

Watching. Speculating. As an old reporter *and* the editor, I feel I've had to stay *on* the fence professionally, though. I love Partonville. Like you, I have mixed emotions, I guess. I'm beginning to think it's time to write an editorial, just to engage the townsfolk in a little dialogue. Stir things up a bit. Broaden the conversation. Make it bigger than Harry's. Yup, that oughta get those letters to the editor pouring in. Find out what folks are *really* thinking. Been too quiet around here lately anyway. I just know things don't stay the same, and Partonville is prime for being picked off."

"Not if *I* have anything to say about it, we're not!" Acting Mayor Gladys McKern nearly startled them both off their stools. He stared at her for a moment, wondering how long she'd been listening. *And the one thing we can be sure of is that* you will *have* plenty *to say, Ms. Mayor!*

Katie blew her nose on yet another tissue Pastor Delbert handed her from the box on his desk. She had cried uncontrollably for no less than five minutes, then spent the next five idling down between sniffs and nose blows and quiet apologies. Pastor would hand her a tissue. She'd blow. Sigh. Sniff. Dorothy would hold her hand out, Katie would place the tissue in it, and then Pastor would hand Katie another tissue as the tears once again flowed.

Nellie Ruth had peeked in once. Being highly tuned in to spiritual matters, she immediately surmised God at work, backed out around the corner, bowed her head and recalled, with clarity and a surprise gust of emotion, her own first adventure on these grounds. Prayers leapt right and left. Prayers of thankfulness for her own healing so long ago and prayers for God to be present and real in Katie's life now.

"I'm sorry," Katie uttered in a hushed tone time and again. Those around her simply listened and continued the tissue assembly line. Josh watched in awe, swallowing hard himself many times. His heart was racing as he was unsure what might follow.

"There is never a need to apologize for tears, Katie," Dorothy finally said. "It looks to me, child of His, like you've had a whole lot bottled up in there for a very long time. Crying is just what you needed to do, Lord knows."

Katie looked up at Dorothy, who had moved around next to Pastor to talk to her. The look on Katie's face was somewhat helpless yet quizzical. Dorothy gazed at Katie, searching from the top of her head to her eyes and her red nose, on down to her hands clenched around a tissue in her lap. Then back into her eyes.

"Yes. The Lord knows. And I believe you do, too. For everything there is a season, and today was crying time."

Katie's eyes darted down toward her hands that were now wringing one another. Dorothy had this way of seeing too much. More, perhaps, than Katie herself was aware of. For the first time in her life, Katie was not only unable but also disinclined to crust over and take command. She was simply too perplexed, as well as drained.

A long, motionless silence ensued.

Katie finally cleared her throat. It looked like the floods had concluded and that she was ready to move on with the task at hand. In a moment of transition, Pastor looked at his watch, then stiffly got up off his knees and offered Katie his hand to help her out of the chair.

"I think it's time we go upstairs and finish the arrange-ments. I imagine Nellie Ruth is wondering what happened to us!" Just then, a scuffling of feet could be heard outside the door, followed by the faint sound of footsteps running up the stairs. Dorothy grinned at Katie, an all-knowing grin. Katie was embarrassed to think that anyone else witnessed this whatever it had been.

"Yes, Pastor Delbert. We need to get things in order. Josh and I haven't even been by Aunt Tess's yet. We've got to pick up a key from the lawyer's office, and I was hoping we might settle up and dispose of her belongings in the next few days before we leave. I also need to speak with a Real-tor. I'd like to get the place on the market in short order."

Pastor Delbert and Dorothy exchanged glances that didn't go unnoticed by Katie. Neither of them, however, said a word. Instead, they silently began to file out of his of-fice, up the stairs and into the sanctuary, where Nellie Ruth fussed with some flowers she obviously had not been ar-ranging. Within ten minutes or so, everything seemed quite in order for the evening's wake and tomorrow's funeral. At least in as good order as anything could be under such out-of-order circumstances.

Katie finally found a parking spot across the square from where Rick Lawson's second-floor office was housed, "right above Hornsby's Shoe Emporium," Nellie Ruth had told her upon leaving the church. Unfortunately, she and Josh had to walk right past Harry's to get there, and it made her bristle again. Although a bit of an inexplicable hollow long-ing had surfaced inside her in the church, whatever—and she did mean *whatever*—had transpired in church was now forgotten in a resurgence of the memory that she was, in-deed, in Pardon Me Ville. She glared in the window as they hustled by, as if to send the gawkers a message. All she saw, however, was the reflection of her own self glaring back.

They found the doorway with RICK LAWSON, ATTORNEY AT LAW printed on it in block letters just to the left of Hornsby's Shoe Emporium. Josh pulled open the door for his mom, and they went up the creaky, narrow stairway.

Rick Lawson's secretary greeted them and took them into Mr. Lawson's office, a ten-by-ten mess. Papers and file folders sat in disheveled piles everywhere, some piles more than two feet tall, including one on his desk. File drawers were open, and files were stacked on top of them. The two green vinyl chairs in front of his desk had stacks of paper on them, and he was leaning over one holding a pile in each hand, obviously caught in the act of attempting to clear the decks for their arrival. He was quite a mess himself, wearing very worn, pin-striped, shiny wool pants a couple sizes too big held up by suspenders that were too long and that sagged across a blue-and-white striped shirt with frayed cuffs.

"Mr. Lawson?" Katie asked.

"Yes. Yes."

"Kathryn Durbin."

"Come in, please," he said as he stacked the piles in his hands, one atop the other, set that stack on top of the stack on one of the chairs, then picked the growing bundle up and set it atop the stack on the other chair. He paused, patted the ever-growing stack, then extended his arms and scooped his fingers underneath the pile. He set his chin down on top of the entire mess, picked it up, turned this way and that searching for an empty spot before finally depositing the wad on the front corner of his desk, right next to the other two-foot pile. Katie figured this is probably how the original stack had developed in the first place.

"Won't you have a seat?" he said, casually pointing toward the now empty chairs as if he and they had been ready all along.

Katie gave the chair seat a quick glance, swiped at it with her hand, then realized she was too tired to care about either her silk pants or the remaining dust bits. Josh sat beside her, and they both watched Mr. Lawson begin raking his fingers up the side of one of the stacks until swiftly, like a magician snatching a tablecloth out from under the dishes, he yanked out a folder that said "Walker" on the file tab. He sat down at his desk and set the file on top of whatever papers were already spread before him, took a deep breath, then opened the file with what seemed like rather dramatic ceremony given the mess he sat in.

"Ah, yes. You're Katie Durbin, Tess Walker's last living relative. We've already figured that out now, haven't we?"

"Yes, we certainly have." Having, within the last hour or so, just discovered the deep emotional truth of that, she quickly moved on to the business at hand. "I'm here to pick up Aunt Tess's house key, Mr. Lawson."

"So you are," he said with a tone in his voice that smacked of a Charlie Chan detective movie. "So you are." Josh actually snickered out loud, then pretended he was clearing his throat when Katie's head snapped in his direction.

Mr. Lawson flipped a few papers over in the file and produced an envelope. "Ah, here we go then. Just what we're looking for." He opened the envelope and extracted a key that was tied lanyard style to a piece of worn, dirty lace. Katie couldn't believe her eyes. "A skeleton key!" she said louder than she'd intended, especially since she didn't intend to respond out loud at all.

"Cool!" Josh uttered.

Mr. Lawson then produced a piece of folded paper from within the envelope and read a hand-scrawled note. Then he folded the paper back up, redeposited it into the envelope and said, "Just the way the Partonville police found it, Ms. Durbin. It was tied around your aunt's neck at the time of her death."

"Police?" Katie asked.

"Yes. I'm sure you know the police have to be phoned when someone is found dead in their home, and an autopsy has to be performed, just to make sure there is no foul play."

"Foul play!" Katie spat. "Someone suspected foul play? No one mentioned any such thing to me, Mr. Lawson."

"It's simply a matter of the law, Ms. Durbin. You can be sure Mac followed proper procedure to the letter of the law, ma'am."

"Mac?" Katie asked.

"Sergeant McKenzie Phillips, Ms. Durbin. Townsfolk just call him Mac."

"And I am to assume everything was found in order? The hospital told me she died of natural causes."

"Yes, of course. Everything was perfectly normal, aside from the fact she was dead."

Katie's head reared back a little, she raised her eyebrows and looked at Josh, who was clearly stifling a grin. She had to admit that this entire place seemed to be a bit of a joke. If she hadn't been so tired and stressed, she might have laughed herself.

"I am giving you this key, Ms. Durbin, not exactly in accordance with the letter of the law, as all the proper documentation hasn't been completely signed and filed. However, since your aunt was wise enough to contact me upon the death of your mother ten years ago in order to put her entire estate in a trust, and since her entire estate is worth very little, which is good because there will be nothing for probate, and"–he leaned forward at this point–"begging your pardon but we're talking reality here"–he sat back in his chair–"I rest assured, knowing you are the sole successor trustee named in her trust, that you are indeed in charge of everything located in that house on Vine Street and that everything your aunt owned is in it. And I do mean everything, Ms. Durbin."

Katie stared at him blankly, trying to sort through a sentence that seemed to have no beginning or end. For a brief moment she wondered if he looked and sounded like this in a courtroom and was glad to know she wouldn't have to find out.

"Have you seen inside your aunt's house lately, Ms. Durbin?"

"I have not been to her home since before my mother died, Mr. Lawson. But I do know at that time she was a bit of a pack rat."

"I'd say you're in for a shock then, Ms. Durbin, so you might want to get a bite of lunch before you go." With that he handed her the key. As she was about to stand up he asked her to remain seated for a moment while he got out her copy of the trust, which he immediately started tossing folders around to unearth. He said he suspected that she wouldn't be able to locate the original copy perhaps for quite some time since Tess Walker kept it in her house and, "well, that is definitely going to be a project." *Pretty funny words coming from someone whose office looks like* this, Katie mused.

Miraculously, he found the rubber-banded stack, handed her the copy and then walked them to his office door.

"I'm sorry I can't make the wake tonight. I don't mean to be disrespectful, but I've got softball practice. I'll see you at the funeral tomorrow, though," Mr. Lawson said as they parted ways.

Josh swallowed down his shock, not at the fact that the lawyer couldn't attend the wake, but softball? The guy had to be seventy-five years old if he was a day.

12

Aunt Tess's house was on Vine Street, three blocks off the square. As Katie turned onto Vine off Main, she had another flashback. She recalled always thinking that the houses on Vine Street were smaller than anywhere else in town. Today's experience was no different.

Although each home had a unique structure, color and layout, they all were wood frame with a brick chimney on one side or the other. Some had odd room additions stuck on this way and that. They each had approximately the same size yard and were decidedly sparse in terms of aesthetics. Rather sad-looking.

She crept along with the windows down, listening to the silence. She couldn't remember a time when their street in the city was so quiet. It was, in fact, somewhat unnerving, making her realize how conditioned, perhaps numbed, to the sounds of cars and sirens and televisions and conference calls and commotion she was.

Suddenly the squealing sounds of a car came around the corner behind her, knocking her out of her reverie. She looked into her rearview mirror to see the front grille of a very large white, beat-up Lincoln racing toward the backside of her SUV. Before she could turn her head to get a better look, the car and the flapping ears and windblown tongue of a funny-looking dog with its head out the window flashed by her, its driver all but running the car up on the lawns. As quickly as the car had passed her by, it zinged in front of her, pulling up toward the end of the block, then jerking to a stop in front of her.

"Take cover!" Josh hollered. "Grandma's on the loose!"

Katie hit the brakes and pulled over. She realized she was nearly in front of Aunt Tess's house anyway, so she just parked her vehicle. Before she could open her own door, out of the Lincoln popped Dorothy Wetstra. She positioned herself at her rear side window, spread her legs to steady herself, then stuck out her arms. Out the window flew the funny little dog, nearly knocking Dorothy back into the street. Josh laughed out loud. His mother sat there with her mouth agape. It was beginning to sink in that the only thing she could count on while she was in Partonville was the unexpected.

As soon as Dorothy set her on the ground, Sheba came galloping back to greet Katie, who had just swung her legs around to the ground. Up onto her slacks Sheba jumped, tongue and tail wagging, mindless of the dusty paw prints she pranced all over peach silk.

"Sheba Wetstra!" Dorothy yelped. "Why, that is no way to behave!" Katie tried to hold Sheba down while acting as if that wasn't what she was doing. "Nice Sheba," she said through her teeth while trying to grab her collar.

Josh had sprung around the car. He scooped Sheba up to his face, which Sheba immediately began to lick and lap. Katie was still dusting off her pants when Dorothy caught up to her.

"I'm sorry about that, Katie. Sheba loves everybody, and I'm afraid she just doesn't have manners when it comes to being a greeter."

"It's quite all right," Katie lied, working to be polite to this woman who had so graciously seen her through whatever it was she had gone through this morning.

"I decided you shouldn't have to go into that house alone, Katie dear. I phoned Rick and he told me you were on your way here."

"Josh is with me. I'm not alone."

"I know, but honestly, I fear you might be in for more than you expected."

Josh set Sheba down, and she took off running for the yard, where they all watched her disappear into foot-tall swaying grasses. It was the first time Katie had noticed the horrid tangle of a yard.

"Oh!" was all she could get out. Josh walked up beside his mom and said, "What next? This is turning out to be quite the day! Looks like we should have brought a machete with us, Mom!"

Katie just stood there staring. Her shoulders slumped forward. No wonder everyone had been throwing each other glances. Rick Lawson had tried his best to warn her. She was beginning to dread unlocking the door, if this was a hint of things to come.

"I'm afraid your Aunt Tess didn't handle things very well these last many years, dear, although I understand she did manage to keep her bills paid and feed herself. People just never saw her out and about. The reason they knew she was okay was because they'd see her lights go on and off at night, and she called in grocery orders to Your Store, handing them a check when they delivered. Other than that, she just kept entirely to herself. I suppose someone told you that's how they discovered her, right? She didn't answer the door when they came with her groceries. It just wasn't like her. Eventually the sheriff was called. Her door was un-locked, thank goodness, so they didn't have to do any dam-age. They discovered her in her bed, where she must have gone to lie down after phoning in her order."

Over the last couple days, Partonville residents had pieced together a few facts, and Gladys McKern had been eager to share with Dorothy any inside info she had gleaned as mayor. Of course, Gladys also wanted everyone to notify her the minute Katie Durbin gained entry to her aunt's house. *Gladys is the last thing Katie needs right now,* Dorothy thought.

Katie didn't say a word as she began fumbling through her purse for the key. Once she had it in her hand, she walked toward the rusting metal gate that swung open into the yard, even though there was no fence. The tall grasses had nearly covered over the cracked and heaving sidewalk. Katie made her way toward the door, Josh right behind and Dorothy bringing up the rear. Sheba was already facing the door, sitting on the sloping cement front porch. Katie stepped up behind her. Sheba didn't even look at her; she just stood up, then began waving her backside and sticking her nose into the space where the door meets the frame, as though she could pry it open.

"I've heard it's quite an awful mess in there, Katie," Dorothy said sympathetically as Katie put the old black key into the lock.

"There's only one way to find out," Josh said.

"One way," Katie said. She twisted the key clockwise un-til she heard a click, then slowly pushed open the door. Since all the window shades were drawn tight and there was no glass in the door, it was too dark to see. She reached her arm around the corner in search of a light switch. Her fingers fumbled over yet another memory from her past: Aunt Tess had push-button light switches! Katie pushed the top button and a dim overhead lightbulb came on. It had no shade. The light cast an eerie glow around the tiny living room. No matter what kind of awful disaster Katie might have expected, she never could have mentally prepared for anything quite as horrible as was revealed in this moment. Rick Lawson's office was nothing but a bit messy compared with this chaos.

Katie gasped aloud. She would have collapsed into a chair had there actually been a place to sit down. Her mind simply couldn't take in all that her eyes were trying to absorb. Josh and Dorothy were speechless themselves until Dorothy muttered, "Lord have mercy on us all."

"Man! I've never seen such a mess," Josh finally said. "And you think *my* room is bad, Mom!"

Katie remembered watching the news on the television one evening. After neighbors complained, Chicago police had discovered a woman and her five children living in conditions that they kept describing on the news as "squalor." Although Katie wasn't sure what the word meant when she first heard it blaring out of her surround-sound speakers, film clips revealed the meaning. Who would have ever guessed that real estate tycoon Kathryn Durbin would have a relative living in those same conditions.

For a moment, Katie felt slightly light-headed again. She reached out her arm and leaned against the wall. Thankfully, however, she slowly began to notice that although everything was everywhere, there was no odor other than that old smell one noticed when walking into an antiques store. There were no moldy dishes of old food sitting around and no piles of dirty diapers as they'd kept showing on TV. No, Aunt Tess's squalor was just piles and piles of clothes and newspapers and books and photographs and linens and pencils and bits of jewelry and . . .

The only way, other than the front door, to get out of the living room was through a narrow passageway that was itself built up on the sides with stuff. Katie cautiously entered into what felt like a labyrinth, bypassed the kitchen, fearing it would be more than she could take, and moved through the masses until she came to Aunt Tess's bedroom. She reached around the corner and punched on the light. Again, she was met with complete disarray. Old wooden boxes and strewn clothes and yet more jewelry and books. Things were even piled on the bed, and it looked as if Aunt Tess had simply curled up in a little nest she'd built around her.

Framed photographs lined the bedroom walls. Pictures of people she didn't know. Faces that stared at her from all directions. She swiftly yet carefully moved back to the bedroom entryway, punched off the light and sidestepped her way back into the hall, where she ran smack into Josh. She let out a loud yelp, then screamed, "Joshua! You scared the life out of me!" He grabbed her arms and said, "Mom, get a grip. It's only me." Mother and son stood face to face. He realized, as he continued to hold her arms, that she was shaking.

"Mom, I'm really getting worried about you. Maybe we better just leave now, find a place to eat and go back to the Lamp Post so you can rest. This has been a . . . a . . . hard morning for all of us."

Katie drew a deep cleansing breath and announced that she would be fine, although she did acknowledge she was feeling a bit weary and edgy. They awkwardly exchanged places in the hallway so they could pass one another.

She peeked in the bathroom, sighed, then said, "I'm going to look in the kitchen before we go. Might as well face most of it so I'm not so startled when we return tomorrow after the funeral. I'll spare myself the back bedroom now—I'll save some surprises," she said sarcastically. "You are right about one thing, I need to eat something and lie down. Just give me another five minutes."

"You're gonna be real surprised when you see the kitchen, Mom."

"Swell."

Katie noticed that a glow from the kitchen light, which either Josh or Dorothy had flipped on, was infiltrating the hallway. She was glad she didn't have to reach around another unknown corner for a switch. She was also astounded at the scene before her when she entered.

Aunt Tess's kitchen was spotless! Nothing was out of place, and not a dish was unwashed. The table was completely cleared aside from three ruffly, floral cloth place mats with table settings on them, including a large, empty water glass for each. A loose bouquet of what appeared to be handpicked flowers sat drooping in the middle of the place settings, a rose-colored pillar candle that had never been lit sat on a saucer and there was a framed picture beside it. It looked as though Aunt Tess had been expecting company. Little prickles ran up the back of Katie's neck.

She picked up the photo to get a better look and froze with shock. It was the same photo of Aunt Tess and her mom standing next to a silo that she'd been viewing at her own kitchen table just days before! Tucked into the lower right-hand corner of the frame was a picture of Katie and Josh standing in Katie's kitchen. Josh looked to be about two years old. Her mother must have taken it and mailed it to Aunt Tess.

Katie stood, staring, eyes welling yet again against her will. She clutched the photo of her mom and Aunt Tess to her breast for a moment as tears streamed down her face. The longing for her mother was so intense it was nearly unbearable. She was powerless to stop the consuming ache and in fact felt strangely drawn into its depths.

Dorothy stood motionless in the doorway from the kitchen to the back porch, witnessing the moment. She stared at Katie's closed eyes and pursed lips. She watched Katie's hand cover the photo held near her heart as Katie began to sway back and forth in a rocking motion.

"Oh, Mother," she whispered. "Mother."

Dorothy couldn't help but see the faint resemblance between mother and daughter, which was most visible in the shape of Katie's face and her wide-set eyes. Clarice used to set her lips together like that when she was upset, Dorothy recalled. But most of all, Dorothy pondered, Katie looked like her tenderhearted father.

Dorothy just stood there in the shadows, not wanting to interrupt the moment, but it didn't last long. Josh bounded into the kitchen holding Sheba. He walked up behind his mom and said, "I think we ought to get a dog, Mom."

Katie spun on her heels, and Sheba quickly leaned forward toward her face and began licking away the tears. Katie was so stunned she yelled at Josh for startling her again. She set the photograph down, asked if the bedroom light was turned off and announced that it was time to go.

After she'd stormed out of the kitchen, he picked up the photograph to see what had captured her attention. It appeared as though the woman on the left could be his grandmother, but he didn't know who the other lady was. Dorothy noticed the look on his face and stepped forward. He held up the photograph and faced it toward her without speaking.

"Of course, the one on the left is your grandmother, Josh. The other, well, meet your Aunt Tess."

13

Dorothy had invited Josh and Katie back to her farm for lunch, but Katie declined, needing some space. Dorothy accepted Katie's refusal but insisted that everyone attending the funeral be invited back to her farm afterward. Although Katie wasn't very keen on the idea, Dorothy's argument finally became persuasive.

"Katie, honey, folks around here are used to being fed after a funeral, usually at someone's home. It's something we not only plan on but also enjoy. Obviously, child, you are not going to invite anyone back to *this* place," she said as she motioned toward Aunt Tess's now locked-up house. "Please let me serve you in this way. We'll just have Pastor make the announcement. Everybody in town knows where I live. There won't be any unnecessary explaining to do. Besides, I enjoy gathering everyone together. It would make me happy to know I helped send off an old friend."

"Come on, Mom. Sounds like a good idea to me. Besides, I've never been on a farm!"

After exploring alternatives in her head, Katie decided to follow Dorothy's suggestion rather than be stuck with a group of Partonvillers waiting like lost sheep, all looking to her for direction. And heaven forbid someone suggest they adjourn to Harry's!

"Okay. I'll take you up on the offer. But I insist I pay for the groceries."

"Deal," Dorothy said, knowing full well that she'd better stop while she was ahead. "Don't worry about a thing. I'll take care of all of it. You can either follow me out to the farm after the services or ride with me and I'll bring you back afterward. I'd love for you both to just pack up your bags and stay with me for as long as you like while you're here finishing your business, but I understand you need your privacy. Besides, I'm happy for Jessica and Paul to have the booking. I'd love to see them make a decent go of that place and reap the rewards for all the hard-work seeds they've sown."

Katie pictured trying to follow Dorothy's speeding bullet of a car. And to ride with her, well, that wasn't a choice! No one should be riding with that woman, not even her own dog! She made a mental note to have Dorothy just give her directions when the time came.

"I'll see you at the wake tonight, honey. I wouldn't expect too many to show up. It's Wednesday. Softball practice. You can count on me, though. I'm just the cheerleader." She walked to her car and flung open the back door. Sheba, who had been sitting patiently at her heels during this discussion, leapt right in. Dorothy folded herself in next, slammed the door, fired up the engine, stomped on the gas and spit roadside gravel every which direction, a few stones pelting the front of Katie's big Lexus. In a flash, she was out of sight.

Josh laughed, then summed up the entire moment in one short sentence: "Ride 'em, cowgirl!"

Katie and Josh arrived at the church at exactly 6:00 P.M., when the wake was to begin. They were surprised to find a dozen people already there, seated in the front pews. It was a bit unusual to have a wake at the church, but the *Partonville Press* and the unofficial grapevine had spread the word about the arrangements. Pastor was standing near the door to greet them.

"Good evening, Katie, Josh." Josh extended his hand, welcoming what he knew would be a hearty handshake.

"Good evening, Pastor Delbert," Katie said. "What time do you have?"

"Six o'clock, straight up," he said after giving his Timex a quick glance. "The older residents like to get to evening events early so they can get home. I'm sorry I didn't tell you. Let's go ahead and start a reception line. Nellie Ruth's had people signing the guest register. She set one out for you in the narthex. Dorothy's up front. She's been watching for you."

Katie walked up the aisle very self-consciously. At business events, she enjoyed making the grand entrance and receiving doting attention. Now, however, she simply felt conspicuous, tardy and overdressed in her green suit, heels and emerald jewelry. She wished that when she'd been packing she hadn't been so caught up in proving she wasn't one of them. Even though she really wasn't, except by bloodline, there suddenly seemed no need to prove it. As they craned their necks to watch her coming toward them—as if she were a bride coming down the aisle—she imagined that they pretty much knew that anyway. When they reached the front of the sanctuary, Dorothy sprang out of her seat to greet them. Katie could hear the murmurs at her back.

"Don't you look beautiful, Katie! You look lovely in

green, just like your mother! I do believe that was her favorite color." Dorothy had once again come through with just what Katie needed. She found herself oddly relieved to be back in the company of this most unusual, if somewhat eccentric, woman.

"And Josh! My, what a handsome rascal you are, all dressed up in a tie with your shoes shined and everything."

"Thanks, Dorothy."

"That's Mrs. Wetstra to you, Joshua," Katie corrected.

"Dorothy, for sure," Dorothy said as she grinned at the teenager before her, who was exactly her same height. "It's Dorothy, and I won't settle for anything else." She directed that statement to Katie and patted her arm. Katie was beginning to understand that there wasn't much use in taking Dorothy on.

By this time, Pastor and his wife had succeeded in ousting everyone seated in the pews and corralled them into a reception line. They were lined up to the right of Dorothy. Katie was again glad for her decision to cremate. She wouldn't have wanted people coming just to see what the town's apparently peculiar woman looked like.

Dorothy greeted people first so she could introduce them to Katie and Josh. At the head of the line stood Gladys McKern. Dorothy drew herself up as tall as she could and grabbed hold of Gladys's hand, which was at the time extended to Katie. Dorothy pulled Gladys toward herself so quickly that she nearly knocked Gladys off balance. She spoke quietly, two octaves lower than usual and with all the power and authority she'd ever claimed.

"Gladys McKern, you give this child a break. I can see the look on your face, and this is not the time for business."

"Dorothy Wetstra, I don't believe it's for you to tell me

when it is or when it isn't time for business. I am, however, annoyed you'd think I'd be so insensitive as to bring business into a wake, let alone the sanctuary!"

"Don't talk so loudly, Gladys. They're liable to hear you." Katie had glanced their way, wondering why Dorothy was holding up the line. Pastor Delbert distracted her for a spell by reiterating once again what a nice job the Floral Fling had done with her order. Katie had noticed on her way down the aisle that there were two other arrangements. She asked Pastor who they were from, and he said Dorothy and the collection pot Lester put out at Harry's. By this time, Gladys was in front of her.

"Gladys McKern, acting mayor," she said. "May I extend my sympathies on behalf of all the residents of Partonville." Gladys handed Katie a card and motioned for her to open it. "May the Lord bless and keep you in this time of sorrow," the card read on the outside. "And hold you right in the palm of his hands as you heal," it read on the inside. It was signed, "Gladys McKern, acting mayor, on behalf of all of Partonville."

"How lovely," Katie forced herself to say. Somehow this felt more like an advertisement for the mayor's office than true sympathy, but then Katie admired anyone who would seize the chance to get in a little PR.

Jessica Joy was next. "Oh, Miss Durbin, again please let me extend my sympathies about your aunt. If there's anything you need while you're here, please let me or Paul know. And this"—she turned to grab the arm of the man behind her and coax him up beside her—"is my husband, Paul. Paul, this is Kathryn Durbin and her son, Joshua."

Paul had his hands stuffed in his jeans pockets. His hair was still wet from a recent combing, his pale blue-and-white plaid shirt was crisply pressed and his eyes only glanced at Katie for a moment. He seemed uncomfortable in her presence. Then again, maybe he was uncomfortable in anyone's presence, Katie thought. She extended her hand. Paul reached for it, gave it one up-and-down shake and said, "Nice to meet you. We're sorry for your loss." He just as quickly shook Josh's hand, then stuffed his hand back in his pocket.

"I'm sorry we can't stay longer," Jessica said sincerely. "We've got to get back to the motel. We're expecting a check-in around seven, and we sure don't want to miss them. I'll see you tomorrow, although Paul has to work. The funeral is at ten, right?"

"Yes," Dorothy, Katie and Josh all responded at the same time.

Immediately Dorothy began greeting the next in line. "Katie Durbin, this is my oldest friend, May Belle Justice, and her son, Earl." Before Katie could extend her hand, May Belle pressed in and gave her a gentle hug. "I'm pleased to meet you, Katie. I wish it could be under happier circumstances. I know Dorothy and Pastor Delbert will take good care of you while you're here. If there's anything I can do to help, please let me know. I imagine you've got your hands full, having to handle all this alone."

"Thank you for your kind offer. I do have my son, Joshua, to help," she said, pointing to her side.

"Well, you're just as handsome as Dorothy told me, Joshua." May Belle turned to face Earl and said to him, "Earl Justice, say hello to Katie Durbin and her son, Joshua."

Earl's eyes never left the floor. He didn't notice either

Katie's or Josh's hands extended in greeting, but then he wouldn't have taken them anyway. A mumbled "Hello" could be heard coming out of his mouth. Katie and Josh said "Hello" back and glanced at one another.

"Earl Justice is a little shy, aren't you, Earl?" Dorothy said. "But he's one of my favorite people in the whole world." Earl looked up at his Dearest Dorothy and his eyes brightened a bit, but he didn't respond.

"Time to go, Earl. Nice to meet you," May Belle said to Katie. "We'll see you tomorrow. I'll be bringing plenty of desserts up to the farm, so please don't worry yourself about anything. You'll learn that although Dorothy isn't the best of cooks, she always makes more than enough." May Belle gave her dear friend a wink, then off they went.

Katie turned to see who was next.

"Arthur Landers," a gruff voice said. "One of Dorothy's neighbors. Didn't know your aunt, really, although we went to school together. Me and my wife both went to school with her. High school, that is," he added, as though a sudden need had come over him to clarify that. "Jessie sends her condolences and says she'll see you tomorrow. She's the captain and pitcher of the Partonville Wild Musketeers. Better than having her throw things at *me*, I guess," he said with a devilish sneer.

"Arthur Landers, now you behave yourself lest you scare our new friends," Dorothy said. "Arthur's really harmless, Josh. He just doesn't act like it. He is, however, the only human alive who can keep The Tank on the road."

"The Tank?" Josh queried.

"That white, dented wreck of a car she drives," Arthur said.

After having witnessed Dorothy and her big bomber of a car in motion, Katie understood why they called it The Tank.

"See ya tomorrow, I reckon," Arthur said. "And the first game is a week from Saturday, if you're still around. We play the Palmer Pirates. You can't miss the ballpark. It's the only thing on the hard road between here and Yorkville."

Josh, having decided that anyone over seventy who looked like they could still move must be playing softball, asked, "Why aren't you at practice, Mr. . . . um . . ."

"Landers."

"Mr. Landers."

"The first time Jessie beaned me with a softball I figured I didn't have to be very smart or dumb to let that happen again. As good an arm as she's got, having played near pro ball in her day, I knew it wasn't no accident."

Josh laughed. Katie realized she'd done the same. It was the first time in a very long time, and it felt good.

Arthur, however, hadn't even cracked a grin.

The rest of the hour-long wake went by quicker than Katie and Josh might have imagined. Pastor Delbert had warned them that an hour would be plenty. They were glad they'd listened, as the last twenty minutes brought no newcomers and nearly everyone else was gone. Dorothy had excused herself and was out of the sanctuary checking on things for the funeral when one last person literally ran in at six-fifty-five. She looked to be about Josh's age, wore dirty jeans and a baseball cap on backward. She shook Josh's and Katie's hands, didn't say who she was, expressed pat condolences, breathlessly said she'd see them tomorrow and that she was sorry she couldn't stay longer but she needed to get back before Musketeer batting practice was over. She left as abruptly as she'd entered, leaving Katie and Josh standing with their mouths agape.

"Mom, if you've got your calendar in your purse, write that ball game down. I have a feeling this could be more interesting than we think! But what's *she* doing on the team?"

"Of course I have my calendar, Josh, but I'm sure not planning on being here that long, although there is an outside possibility now that I've seen the house. I might have to come back without you so we can get you back in school by next week. Maybe I should just hire a demolition team and let them have at it, burying all that stuff in the process. That would probably be the easiest way. I doubt there's anything worth saving. I'm not sure *I'll* live long enough to go through all of it."

Josh gave his mother a peculiar look, one that she couldn't read. "What?" she said. "Why are you staring at me like that?"

"I just thought . . . I just thought . . ."

"What? What are you thinking, Joshua. Speak up!"

Josh recalled his mother's episode in this very basement, then her tears at Aunt Tess's. "I just wondered if you might, um, be glad we came."

"What on earth would make you say *that*?"

"Just a feeling I had. A feeling like maybe . . . I don't know . . . maybe there was something here for us to discover?" Now it was Katie's turn to stare. Thank goodness Dorothy, Nellie Ruth and Pastor Delbert came down the aisle and interrupted this odd conversation.

Final instructions and plans were reviewed. Katie made a mental note to arrive at nine-thirty tomorrow, a half-hour early, so she wouldn't be caught off guard again. Then it was quickly determined that they were all tired, there was a big day ahead of them and it was time to retire for the evening. Oddly enough, Katie couldn't wait to get back to the Lamp Post. Maybe she'd even draw a bath and make use of some of those Avon samples. Yes, that's just what she'd do.

14

Dorothy stood in the loft of the barn, gazing out the doors toward the west and the Landers place; their farm had been passed down through generations, too. Aside from the Landerses' farm buildings and a small grove of trees, as far as the eye could see the view was of what would soon be beautiful straight rows of corn. Dorothy considered the many years of Jessie and Arthur's friendship and wondered what their reaction might have been if she'd told them her dilemma the other day when Arthur was fixing The Tank's door.

She hadn't been able to come up with the right introduction to even a vague conversation to feel them out. Arthur and Jessie, however, would be the first to be directly affected if she sold to Craig & Craig. She hated to think that she might do *anything* to jeopardize such a long-standing and valued friendship. No, sir, the older Dorothy got, the more she valued God's gift of friends and long-lasting marriages.

Suddenly she found herself recalling an amazing story Arthur had shared with her years ago. He'd been working on The Tank in his "garage" and, as usual, they'd been gabbing about this and that while he tightened and tested, tinkered with and fretted over the obstinate "lady."

Eventually the discussion had rolled around to the price

of corn per bushel. Dorothy, never before having asked Arthur about it, queried him as to why he'd ever stopped farming his own land and gone into the automotive business. In her wildest dreams, she would never have expected the answer he delivered—about a lot of things. Obviously, Jessie had been nowhere around for this discourse. She'd have hog-tied him on the spot if she'd ever found out he'd told such a personal tale out of school.

Dorothy had never before, nor had she since, witnessed Arthur being as animated and sometimes even tickled with himself as he was during the telling.

You know I've always been a natural at fixing cars, Dorothy, tinkerin' with them for years as a hobby out in this old toolshed. Well, one day I finally admitted to Jessie—as well as myself—that I hated farming.

"Well, THAT'S just great!" she said, following me across the yard when I stomped away from her. "How do you expect we'd have eaten all these years if your dad hadn't left you this farm and all its equipment?" She was a-hoppin' mad, for sure.

I got just as mad right back at her. I worked up such a head of steam that I confessed I had always *hated farming. Without thinkin', I said, "And not only did I never want to be a farmer, I never really wanted a WIFE either!" Now, keep in mind, Dorothy, it'd been ten years since that crazy night we decided to run away and get hitched!*

"Well, I feel the same way about a HUSBAND!" she screamed. There we were, me stridin' toward this old shed to where I used to come just to get away from her, and her a-chasin' right behind me every stomp of the way. When we entered, screamin' like banshees, chickens went squawkin' and flappin' this way and that.

"So NOW what?" she said to my back as I walked on through the shed to open the back swingin' doors. *"NOW what do you have to say?"*

Well, I turned on my heels and stared at her. I put my hands on my hips and watched her begin to mimic my every twitch. There we stood, just starin' at each other from opposite ends of the shed for probably a good three or four minutes. Two stubborn, hotheaded people. I'll TELL you, we are stubborn!

I realized that although I was angry and had spoken out of turn, I finally felt free, having spoken the truth. Jessie, well she looked like she might get sick on me. Like she was thinkin' the same things I'd been thinkin' all along. We stood there actin' like a blimp blowed in between us and we were studyin' it!

Then it struck me what I needed to do. Without givin' it a lick more thought, I picked up an old piece of plywood, brushed off the dust and propped it against my workbench. Then I rummaged around 'til I found a can of black paint and a brush and I scrawled me some words. Jessie just watched. I finally had to put my hands on her arms and move her two feet to her right so I could reach my ladder. I got my old mayonnaise jar full of nails, stuck a couple between my teeth, set up the ladder right outside the shed door, climbed up carryin' the plywood and nailed my sign above the door. *GARAGE, OPEN FOR BUSINESS,* it said.

Jessie's eyes growed as wide as cow pies, but she didn't say a word. I climbed down the ladder, put everything away and stared at her for a few seconds. Then I said, *"There. That's what I have to say. I'm gonna make a living doing what I do best and what I like most and what I already do for free. I'm gonna call Challie Carter tomorrow and lease him our land. He's been sayin' for years he'd like more farming acres. Now, woman, what do you have to say?"*

"What about us, Arthur?" she asked. *"What about us?"* I tell you, Dorothy, her voice was steely, borderin' on a hiss. So I says, *"I*

reckon we're just stuck with one another, woman. Besides, I'm out of plywood to write US up a new job description."

I stomped out and began to close the shed doors to shut her inside. She raced out in the nick of time, trotted around in front of me, then threw back like she was gonna swing. Why, I just reacted, pulled back my fist, then got a grip on myself and took off again, her racin' behind me. . . . I wasn't sure where I was goin', but I knew I needed to separate myself from her. I might be an ornery old cuss, but I don't hit WOMEN! I headed toward the field, then spotted the old outhouse pappy used to sit in.

I stormed in, closed the door behind me and locked it. She began rattlin' the door and yelpin', "Arthur Landers, you get yourself out here!" I just plopped down on the seat and sat there, staring at her outline through the cracks in the wood. After a spell, she finally stomped away.

Next thing I knew there was a whap up against the side of the outhouse. It liked to scare me . . . I jumped and knocked my head against the back wall. Then Whap! Whap! I couldn't figure out what she was doin'. Then she started yellin' again.

"Arthur Landers, you listen to me." Whap! "I'm glad you're opening a garage. I'm glad you're gonna stop farming because maybe now that sour puss of yours will take on a different shine." Whap! I ducked like a boxer.

"I'm glad we finally spoke the truth to one another," she said. Whap! Whap again!

"And I agree that for better or for worse, we're just stuck with one another. But you're gonna listen to me now, and I've got plenty to say, buster!"

The peltin' stopped for a minute, and I peeked through one of the cracks. Why, that woman was throwing crabapples from her little tree! Must have been the first thing she spied for ammunition. I'll be darned if she wasn't reloading her apron pockets! I knew she still

*had a pickoff arm, and I was the one she was tryin' to pick off!
Why, I knew she could keep at this for hours if she was downright
angry enough, and she surely was—not that I blamed her. And even
as ornery a coot as she was and continues to be, I guess I'd just
kinda grown used to her.*

*Without thinkin', I reached in my overalls and grabbed my good
ol' Hohner harmonica. Then I begun to playin' the "Dark Town
Strutter's Ball" as loudly as I could, fixin' to drown out the whap-
pin'. The more she laid out her complaints and sailed those crabapples, the faster and louder I played! I tell ya, Dorothy, it was
dusk before the tree was out of apples, Jessie was too pooped to
throw and I was out of wind!*

Today, four decades later, they were still married, still argu-
ing, Arthur still playing the harmonica in the outhouse and
Jessie still winging whatever was at hand, including clothespins, rocks and an occasional egg a roosting chicken plunked
down in her sight. The only thing that had changed was
Arthur's garage. One day a few years ago he woke up and
without ceremony removed the sign. It was time to retire.

Time to retire, Dorothy thought. *Arthur knew when it was
time to retire. But when and how does one retire from the place they
were born, even though the burden of it is beginning to wear them
down? How do they know, Lord, whether it's time to fight, surren-
der or simply say good-bye to the past and move on with dignity
while one still can? How does one suddenly put her interests above
her neighbors'—or even know what her neighbors' interests are? Just
as no one suspected Arthur hated farming, maybe I'm misjudging
how people will react to my selling the farm.*

*Or does one just stay until You call them home, letting the next
generation, with their own ideas, figure it all out? Hear me, Lord?*

I'm trusting You for some answers. Oh, if only Henry were here to help me understand all the details in that pile of paper. I need some help with this decision, Lord. And soon.

"Thank You, God, for loving all Your children, even those who don't make it to church on Sunday, for only You know what's truly in our hearts. And Lord, we pray for the continued healing of those who mourn Tessa Martha Walker. Amen!" Pastor Delbert boomed his grand closing finale.

He raised his bowed head and looked once again at the small gathering, his eyes settling on Gladys, who sat square in front of him. She was also eyeballing him a good one.

"Those who take the Lord seriously," she'd been heard saying on many occasions to anyone who would listen, "make their way to church on Sunday morning. And that's that."

Pastor smiled at Gladys, lifted his eyes to address the rest of the sheep and continued.

"Now, Katie Durbin, who I'm sure you all know by now is Tessa Walker's niece from Chicago, has graciously invited us all to lunch. She will be hosting us out at Dorothy's farm. Katie, would you and your son, Josh, please stand up? I believe everyone's had a chance to meet you, but in case they haven't, we want to make sure they know who to pay their condolences to."

Josh sprang out of his seat like he'd been catapulted. Katie didn't budge. Josh leaned down, gently put his hand under her elbow and pretended to be assisting her to stand. She stiffened and rose, happy she'd made the choice to skip some of her accessories today.

"Would you two please turn around so as folks can see you?" Pastor implored.

Josh swiveled right around and gave a quick wave. Katie kind of looked over her shoulder, smiled a lame smile and nodded. Quickly they both were seated.

"I believe you all know where Dorothy's place is, but just in case there is someone here who doesn't, I've prepared a simple map. Nellie Ruth will be handing out copies as you exit. We look forward to seeing you there for some good eats and fellowship."

Thank goodness there's a map! This way it'll be easier to bow out of riding with Dorothy Lead Foot. I have no earthly desire to be buried in this town! Katie lingered in the front pew, allowing those behind her to begin exiting, hoping to postpone as long as possible the engagement of further conversation.

She looked at her watch. It was barely 10:30 A.M., but she was hungry. She'd only had a salad for dinner, and her stomach just hadn't been in the mood for food when she awakened. On the way to the service Josh begged her to stop at a doughnut shop on the edge of town, where he'd pounded down a large orange juice, a small milk and three chocolate-covered doughnuts. The smell of the place gave her the chills. *How could people eat so much sugar so early in the morning,* she wondered.

Pastor finished gathering his notes from the altar, then approached Katie as she was exiting her pew. Simultaneously Dorothy hollered across the sanctuary, "Katie! Josh! You better get out here so we can beat this crowd. It's like a stampede."

"Pastor Delbert," Katie said with an imploring tone of voice, "if you would be so kind as to retrieve a map for us and explain to Dorothy we won't be riding with her. Do assure her we'll be right along."

"Sure. Wait here." He grinned as if sharing an inside joke, turned on his heels and strode over to where Dorothy stood. Josh raced off behind him without saying a word to his mom. When they reached Dorothy, Katie was assured Dorothy accepted whatever Pastor was telling her when Dorothy gave Katie a quick wave and she and Pastor disappeared around the corner.

"I'm riding with Dorothy, Mom! See ya there." Josh didn't wait for a reply, and he, too, left her sight.

By the time Katie trotted across the sanctuary and out into the parking lot, The Tank was already racing away. Sheba's head stuck out the rear window, her tongue flapping in Katie's direction as if to wave good-bye. Although Katie hadn't prayed for years, she found herself asking *someone* to keep an eye on her son.

15

Katie, concerned about Josh riding with Dorothy, was suddenly acutely aware of how much she loved him. The thought of harm coming his way prickled her clear through. Even so, she wasn't used to being with people nearly twenty-four hours a day, and Josh's ability to antagonize and embarrass her was beginning to wear thin. A little space would do her good.

She sat in the parking lot alone in her car, windows rolled down. There was only one other automobile left in the lot, and it was parked where it said PASTOR ONLY. She leaned her head back against the headrest and closed her eyes.

Did I speak to Aunt Tess again after she took Mom's ashes? What an odd thing to be wondering. Knock it off!

A vague image of Aunt Tess began to form in her mind.

What color were her eyes? The same as Mom's? And didn't she used to dye her hair some awful copper color?

"I know this is perhaps awkward timing, but I'd hate for anything to happen to your aunt. Our janitor sometimes is a little hasty about throwing things away."

Katie yelped at the startling intrusion. Right smack in her face was an eight-inch-square cardboard box Pastor Delbert held through the window. The large label aiming right at her forehead said, "Cremated remains: Tessa Martha Walker."

This isn't what I was picturing!

"I'm sorry. I didn't mean to startle you," Pastor said, withdrawing the box so Katie could catch her breath. "I'm afraid it wasn't very sensitive of me to present her right in front of your nose without warning."

Katie reached through the window with both hands, grabbed the box out of his hands and plunked it down on the seat next to her as though it were a bag of groceries.

"No need for apologies. You just startled me." She cranked over the engine. "Will I see you at Dorothy's?"

"I'm afraid not. I've got to work on my sermon, and I have two committee meetings to prepare for. You'll be in the best of hands with Dorothy. I'm sure she and May Belle have everything under control out at the farm. I do hope the service met with your approval."

"Yes. Everything was fine."

"Well, I trust your aunt is home with her Maker now."

No, she's now riding shotgun. "Yes. Yes, I'm sure she is." *Anything to end this conversation and move me one step closer to being done with this day.*

The map was a simple line drawing that served the purpose. Pastor Delbert had laughed when he handed it to her, explaining that everyone else knew where Dorothy lived but at least Katie's need for the map had validated his task. There was only one turn after you exited the church parking lot and got on "the hard road," as Dorothy and Arthur had both called it, toward Hethrow. Pastor had drawn an arrow where the Partonville sign would signal the turn. Katie got stuck driving behind a tractor and didn't see the sign until it was time to turn. She zipped around the corner, sending Aunt Tess careening into the passenger door before she could reach out and grab her.

She pulled over to the side of the road and slammed the car into park. Leaning across the seat, she ever so gently picked up the box, fearing ashes would spill out onto her leather seats. She was relieved to discover it was still tightly sealed, and felt a bit guilty she'd handled the ashes so harshly to begin with.

"That's it, though," she said rather sternly to the box. "You're still not behaving very well." She got out of the car and put Aunt Tess securely on the floor behind the driver's seat.

"Katie Mabel Carol Durbin," she addressed herself out loud, "you're starting to act like you belong in Pardon Me Ville, talking to a box like that. Snap out of it!"

After about a half mile, the road made a bend to the left. She noticed a farm in the distance. A quick check of the map noted Dorothy's as being a half mile past the first farm on the left, so she sped up a bit until pelting gravel got her attention and she backed down her speed. Dorothy'd already done enough ding damage.

Katie spied the outline of a subdivision on the horizon, perhaps a couple miles to the east. *I wonder what this'll go for an acre when progress marches down the road? There's certainly enough land here to pad someone's wallet and slam-dunk the development competition.*

Furrows of promised corn ran this way and that. The patchwork reminded her of the quilt her mom used to tuck her in with when she was little. Clarice told Katie that her grandmother had made it for her before she was born. It was hand-pieced and stitched in greens and browns with an occasional blue square. *I wonder if the quilt might have reminded Mom of this countryside. After all, she was born and raised here until she was, what? Twenty-something when she moved to Chicago? I wonder what ever happened to that old quilt?*

Katie's mom had tried to give it to her when she moved into her own place after college. "Mom, I'm not a child anymore. What do I want with that raggedy old thing?" She could still see the wounded look in her mother's eyes. Her mom had simply said, "Of course, honey. But I'll keep it just in case you ever want it for one of your own children. You might change your mind someday." Clarice had then clutched the quilt to her bosom and hugged it as if it were a child. *I don't remember running across that old quilt when I went through Mom's things.*

Suddenly Katie was well past that first farm, having lost track of how far she'd traveled. A long row of hedge apple trees met the road about a half mile in front of her. That must be the place. *Pastor said I wouldn't be able to see the farmhouse or buildings from the road because they were blocked by a row of trees that lined the driveway.*

She approached slowly, then pulled across the road up to the mailbox, which read "Wetstra." *Now I get it! Wetstra like* wet straw *but without the* w *on the end. Right.* Even though not another vehicle was in sight and she was within a foot of her turn, out of habit she flipped on her blinker.

The trees lined both sides of the long driveway, and a center row of short grass grew between the well-worn gravel tracks. It reminded her of something she'd once read in a novel years ago, back when she had time for fiction. She took her foot off the gas and just allowed the car to move forward at a slow, idle pace. She opened the moon roof, came to a complete stop and just stared up into the fluttering leaves that were growing toward their adult size for the season.

A gust of wind caused the branches to sway and dance and tousled her hair as it blew through the car. Because the graceful arms of the ancient trees on either side of the drive met, folding their fingers together across the sky, they seemed to sail up and down as one delicately knit archway when the gentle winds blew, lifting, falling, swaying. . . .

She became oddly soothed by their rhythms, cradled in their magical spell. Senses quickened, a long-forgotten time from her childhood sprang forth from her memory portfolio.

Katie stood staring at the tent she'd fashioned out of flowered sheets that she'd draped over her mom's clothesline and anchored to the ground with baseball-sized rocks. She then began creating the most dramatic doors at each end with scarves from her mother's bureau drawer, thoughtfully clothespinning each scarf along the angles of the sheets and allowing the bottom edges to trail softly on the ground. Each scarf a different color and pattern, each bright and beautiful and smelling of her mom's sachet.

Finally, when every angle and color combination was just right—and some combinations took a few tries—she lay down faceup, precisely in the middle. The winds blew through her tent, billowing the sheets so that the entire shelter ever so slightly lifted and settled back onto the line, as though they were breathing breaths of kaleidoscoping colors, scarves twirling and dancing in the wind, waving at the universe.

She opened her eyes and for another moment hid in this long tunnel of fluttering green.

What happened to the girl so in love with colors and magic? "Are you in there, Katie girl?" she said aloud. At last she sighed, blinked herself back into full reality and, with a heart that was light and at the same time heavy, slowly drove up the lane.

What she saw when the trees to the right finally ended was an old, two-story white farmhouse with a brick chimney running up the side near the driveway. A graceful, wraparound front porch already had several folks sitting and standing on it, sipping beverages, holding plates and chatting.

The gravel drive curved around behind the house, and Katie followed it. She drove past the chaos of cars that were parked on both sides and up in the backyard. The Tank was pulled right up to the back door of the porch. The driveway veered toward the left and ran right into the lower level of a giant barn. She pulled over and parked just outside the entry to the left of the barn, unbuckled her seat belt, drew two deep breaths and exhaled loudly through her mouth, then opened her car door.

As her eyes panned down the side of the barn they locked on a tall structure. *Surely it can't be!* She stepped out of the car and backed up a bit for a larger view. The sun streaked over the roof of the barn into her eyes, nearly blinding her. She walked across the grass to get into the shade and allowed her vision to adjust. Her heart began racing and her head shook back and forth as goosebumps raced up her arms. *Oh, my!* There, like a giant looming over her, arose the very silo by which her mom and Aunt Tess stood side by side in that photo! What was it about that photo that kept inviting yet unsettling her?

"This place is really something, isn't it, Mom?" Josh said to the back of her head.

Katie screeched and involuntarily jumped back into him, trouncing on the top of his foot with her heel.

"Yow, Mom! Get a grip! You might have drilled a hole right through my Doc Martens!" he said as he hopped around on his right leg while holding his left foot in his hands.

Her heart was now racing so fast she could not get a word out. She just stood there staring at him a moment, then returned her gaze to the silo. Then back at him again. Then back at the silo. *It's as though that photo were talking to me!* Her eyes were open as wide as her lids would allow, and the color had drained from her face.

Josh finally stopped hopping around, stood behind her and looked in the direction in which she was now silently staring.

"Never seen a silo before?"

"Joshua . . . Joshua."

"Yes."

"Joshua."

"Mom! Is your record stuck?"

"Joshua," she repeated again as she turned to face him, "please show me inside."

"All right," he said, taking a moment to search his mom's face. "We were beginning to wonder if you'd gotten lost. Dorothy said she was about to send out a search party."

"When have you ever known me to get lost?" she asked as she walked behind him. "I spent half my career finding places to which people gave me directions." Josh didn't respond; he just kept walking up the drive and around The Tank until they reached the back entryway to the house.

He opened the old, creaking screen door for Katie. *For goodness sake! Is that an actual spring?* Out of real estate habit she mentally recorded it, even though her mind continued to dwell on that framed photo displayed on Aunt Tess's set table, appearing reverently placed next to that photo of her and Josh. *That set table, waiting for whom?*

After taking a few steps across the small back porch enclosure, she walked up four wooden steps. The door separating the porch and the kitchen was already standing open. The kitchen was quite large, spanning the entire back of the house. The cabinets were painted white and had crosshatched glass windows in them. Not many dishes remained in the cabinets, since most of them were stacked on the counter. People were filing along, picking up the flower-trimmed plates, then grabbing a packet of silverware that had been wrapped in a napkin. How on earth Dorothy had managed to have this buffet table ready, warmed and set up before Katie arrived was beyond her. Katie was a wreck for days before company, which she seldom invited for that reason. Plates were piled high with sliced ham, sweet potatoes and green beans.

May Belle beckoned folks to continue on over to the perpendicular counter, where she handed them a dessert plate and asked which of the four delicacies they'd like. "Peach cobbler, double chocolate brownies, gingersnap cookies or tapioca pudding?"

While Katie stood taking all this in, Josh charged past her and marched over to Dorothy, who was fiddling with something at the sink.

"Hey, Dorothy! Where's my plate I asked you to save?"

"Right here, young man. I just washed it up for round two. No sense startin' with what appears to be a plate of slobbers!"

"Thanks, Dorothy!" Back into line he went.

Dorothy noticed Katie standing by the door. She tossed the dish towel over her shoulder, then wiped her hands down the front of her apron.

"Welcome to Crooked Creek, Katie, honey. You must be starved." She grabbed hold of Katie's hand and whisked her right up to the front of the line. "Pardon us, please. Our guest of honor and host has arrived, and if she waits for all of you hungry hounds, there's likely to be nothing left!" Everyone laughed at what they knew to be Dorothy's good humor, although personally Katie didn't think it was very funny. She was in fact embarrassed by the attention.

"Honestly, Dorothy, I'm not that hungry."

"Nonsense! You're nothing but skin and bones, and you've got plenty to do the next few days, so you better keep up your energy!" Before Katie could say another word, Dorothy picked up a plate, stabbed a giant slice of ham and topped it with a pineapple ring. Then she added a medium scoop of sweet potatoes and a healthy helping of green beans and handed her the laden plate. May Belle instantly flanked Katie to the left and escorted her to the dessert counter.

"I hope I've selected something you like, dear. I suspected you were a chocolate lover, and I just happened to have all the ingredients at hand for these double chocolate brownies. Of course, from the looks of me," she said while patting her own stomach with both hands, "I guess you can imagine I like all of them!"

"Now, don't be modest, May Belle," Dorothy chirped. "Go ahead and tell her that's your personal recipe for double chocolate brownies that won the blue ribbon at the county fair last year. Come to think of it, I guess you don't need to do that, since I just did."

Katie wasn't quite sure what to say, other than to admit she really did like chocolate. It just seemed that to begin explaining that she tried to stay away from it because of the caffeine would take too much energy.

"Mom, these brownies *rock*," Josh said, snatching two of them and piling them on top of his already full plate. He disappeared back into the living room as quickly as he'd zipped into the kitchen.

"I'm afraid my son is doing a poor job with his manners today," Katie sighed. It occurred to her that she'd been doing a lot of sighing the last two days.

"He's a beautiful child, Katie, such a good-looking and kind boy! You must be very proud of him." As soon as the words were out of Dorothy's mouth she rushed back over to the buffet line to slice more ham.

Katie looked at Josh through the doorway. She studied his profile as he talked to Rick Lawson, the lawyer, who appeared to be wearing the same rumpled and ill-fitting clothes he had on the other day. As she watched Josh's animated self interact with Mr. Lawson, nodding his head and talking between bites of food, she considered what a long time it had been since she'd really studied him. He was, as

Dorothy had said, a good-looking boy who looked exactly like his father. In fact, she thought as she watched him, he even had some of the same mannerisms. This might have been a good thing, had Katie not been so wounded by Bruce. She had finally crusted over, willing herself to despise the man who had betrayed her. "Kind," Dorothy had said about her son. *Hmmm. Kind.*

Katie noticed Josh suddenly looking to Mr. Lawson's left and followed his gaze. He had spotted that young girl who'd run in and out of the church so quickly last night. This morning, however, she was wearing a pair of navy slacks and a short-sleeved, light green sweater set. Her hair was very blond, shiny and straight. It draped neatly over her shoulders, aside from a few pieces that were pulled back and held in place by a petite gold barrette. When Katie looked back at Josh, she noticed he now seemed to have a difficult time keeping eye contact with Mr. Lawson.

Josh and a girl. Now, there's a new thought.

A hand whomped down on Katie's right shoulder, nearly sending her pineapple slice flying. A booming voice said, "Well, here you are. Katie Durbin, this here's my wife, Jessie Landers." Jessie extended her hand and waited for Katie to jostle her dessert plate to the counter so she could shake. She had yet to have a bite of anything. Jessie pumped her hand so vigorously it made her entire body shake.

"Pleased to meet you, Miss Durbin. I'm sorry about your loss. Can't say as I really knew your aunt, but nevertheless, I'm sure she was a fine woman."

Katie finally placed Arthur Landers and recalled his baseball tale from the night before.

"Thank you. Arthur told me you play baseball and you have quite an arm," Katie said.

Jessie shot Arthur a crooked glance, wondering what all he might have rambled on about. "I hope you'll forgive me for missing the wake, but I knew I could come meet you today and pay my respects. We've got us a big game coming up. If I miss practice, my arm just isn't what it oughta be on game day. And since this is the first of the season, we're still sorting out positions and getting back into shape."

"How long have you been playing?" Katie asked for lack of anything else to say.

"I reckon you could say all my life and not be lying," she said, then chuckled.

"Yessiree, that would be the truth, woman!" Arthur said. "Why, Jessie here played semi-professional ball in her heyday. She earned herself a golden glove in forty-two! Not only did she have the best pickoff arm of any catcher in any league—pegging off more runners trying to steal second base than any other catcher of her time—but she could catch just about anything ever throwed her way, including me."

Arthur laughed. Jessie did not. Katie just stared. The uncomfortable mix of responses didn't hamper Arthur's rambling in the least, although it did cause Katie's eyes to shift away for a moment in hopes she might spot Josh while Arthur continued to rattle on. Instead, her eyes landed on the girl who'd so fascinated Josh. She was now speaking to someone wearing one of the most preposterous outfits Katie had ever seen at a funeral.

It was Maggie Malone, and the girl was Shelby, her oldest great-grandchild. Although Shelby was about as opposite to her great-grandma as they come—a tomboy with a conservative approach to dress—she loved being with her Grammie M and shared her zest for life. Shelby wasn't afraid to tackle anything, including becoming the catcher for the Wild Musketeers.

Shelby had tried out for catcher of the high school team but didn't make it. When she found out through Maggie that the Wild Musketeers were without a catcher—no one's knees were now good enough to get them up out of the squat—she told Grammie M she'd like to catch for them. Ralph McAllister had stepped in as catcher for a season, but the Wild Musketeers got their pants licked in just about every game, since he refused to play with his glasses on and he couldn't see an entire steer without them, let alone the ball covered with its hide. By a unanimous vote he was ousted—first ever ousting on the team—and the winter season found them scouting. The year Jessie toppled over twice leaning out behind the plate was the year she hung up her catcher's mitt and traded it in for the pitcher's warm-up jacket. After all, she still had an arm, as could be proven by the outhouse pelting ritual if nothing else. In fact, Arthur'd even drawn a target on the side of his refuge, just to give her some practice when she was mad.

Maggie tried to explain that not just the team but the entire *league* was made up of oldsters, but Shelby just wouldn't take no for an answer. "Age doesn't matter, and besides you're more fun than most of my friends anyway!" was her determined response. She asked her Grammie M to find out if the "age thing" was a habit or a rule. When Maggie phoned the league coordinator and asked about any rules they might have as to what qualified a player, he answered with just what she was hoping for.

"Mags, we've never found a need to print something official since this is just a friendly competition."

Friendly my foot, she thought. This *is* softball *and reputations are on the line!* What had begun as a friendly, after-the-fish-fry habit had developed over the years into first a challenge from a neighboring fish-fry group, then another, then next thing you know there was a makeshift league. Eventually games were moved to Saturdays to accommodate travelers, records were kept, and one year people began throwing money in a John Deere cap for trophies. Just because only oldsters had signed up for the games didn't mean youngsters couldn't. And that was that. Shelby was in.

For two years she'd been one of their key players, but not without conditions. After her first appearance and a protest from most of the competition, the league, finding it had no such rule about age, took a vote and decided that although she could catch and bat, she would be required to have pinch runners. All things considered, speed needed to be equalized to, well, slow.

Katie excused herself from Arthur and Jessie and moved through the room to get a better look at Maggie's outfit, which consisted of black spandex pants with little slits at the ankles *(Is that a tattoo!),* a fluffy white sweater with a huge cowl neck, a leopard print belt, dangling earrings and a large black straw hat.

And suddenly Katie was caught staring by the person to whom her incredulous eyes were attached. She reached for her other plate, again holding a plate in each hand in order to divert her eyes and once again disengage herself from any more aggressive hug and shake attacks.

"Oh, I bet you haven't met Miss Durbin yet, have you?" Shelby asked when she noticed Maggie and Katie now staring at one another.

"Why, no, I haven't."

By this time Katie had mustered a smile. "We're very sorry for your loss," Maggie said. She then stabbed a forkful of food, green beans first and last with a bit of sweet potato sandwiched in the middle, shoveled it in through her deep mauve painted lips, gave a couple quick chews and swallowed. "And thank you for hosting such a lovely gathering. I was simply famished," she said.

Maggie turned to Shelby. "Shelby, would you please get Grammie's card case from my purse? I left it on the floor over there. I'd like to give Miss Durbin one of my business cards." While Shelby began thrashing through the giant brown leather bag with jewels dangling from the zipper, Maggie continued.

"Miss Durbin, as a token of my sincere sympathies and since I didn't send flowers, I'd like to extend to you a free wash and set at my salon. The card will have the address, but everyone in town knows where La Feminique Hair Salon & Day Spa is located. We're only a block off the square. Just phone ahead, and I'll squeeze you in. I'm pretty booked Thursdays through Saturdays, but I'll come early or stay late if I have to so I can accommodate you while you're in town."

Maggie studied Katie's hair, then plopped her fork on her plate and plucked at a couple of strands on the top of Katie's head. "It looks like you could use a good touch-up, too. I'd just charge you ten dollars for the color." Katie instinctively reared back her head. "Oh, I'm sorry to scare you like that. I imagine your nerves are about spent by now."

"You have no idea," Katie said.

Shelby had finally retrieved Maggie's card case. It appeared to be made out of sterling silver and was beautifully monogrammed with a very ornate *MM*. Shelby held it out in front of her grandmother, then, with her thumb, flipped back the lid like a Zippo lighter. Maggie fingered a card right out and extended it toward Katie, who had no hands to receive it. Shelby grabbed it and, without asking permission or indicating what she was going to do, stuck it in Katie's suit pocket. Katie was beginning to feel like a helpless mannequin being plucked at and invaded like this.

"For goodness sakes!" Dorothy said, coming up to them. "This poor child hasn't had a chance to eat a bite of her dinner, what with us all talking her ear off. Come on, honey, and follow me back into the kitchen. I'm gonna sit you down at the table."

"Really, I'm doing just fine," Katie replied. But before she knew it, Dorothy had whisked the plates out of her hands.

"Follow me, missy, and don't look left or right. Just follow." Katie felt not only at the mercy of Dorothy Wetstra but as though she were traveling in her back draft as well. Truth be known, she was happy to be rescued.

Dorothy pulled out the kitchen chair for Katie and arranged her plates in front of her, but not before getting out a ruffly place mat from one of the giant wooden drawers that lined the cabinets. Without asking, she also served her a large glass filled with water and a lemon slice. "I always take lemon in my water, I hope you don't mind. My fingers just kind of grab for the lemon without thinking."

"Thank you. I always ask for lemon in my water, too. In fact, I order it in diet colas. I can't remember who got me started on that one. I always figure a little vitamin C can't hurt." Katie took a few big gulps of the water and realized how parched she'd become.

"Josh tells me you lead a very busy life."

"Oh?"

"He liked to talk my ear off on the way out here. He said you sell homes?"

"Actually, I deal in commercial real estate, not home sales. It's been a long while since I've shown a house."

"But you used to sell homes though, right?"

"Yes. I've sold my share of properties."

Dorothy paused, waiting to see if Katie would mention her current unemployment. It didn't seem proper to bring it up herself, even though Josh seemed to feel quite free mentioning it on the ride over. In fact, Dorothy thought he almost sounded a little bit happy about Katie's recent canning. She remembered thinking how out of place his response seemed to be, considering the situation.

"So what's your plan for tomorrow? I imagine you've got quite the agenda if you're planning on settling things as quickly as possible."

"I guess Josh and I will try to scrounge up some boxes and begin plowing through all those piles. Can you tell me where might be my best chances for finding boxes?"

"Well, there's Your Store, the local grocery place just a few blocks from your aunt's house. That would probably be the best bet. Nellie Ruth's the assistant manager, and she could scout and save some for you. Or you could try Richardson's Rexall Drugs on the square. I doubt they'd have any big ones, since they deal mostly in little pills." She chuckled at her own humor. "How about I rally a few of the Hookers, and we collect the boxes and come by and help you get started? I imagine it must be overwhelming to even know where to begin."

"Hookers?" Katie nearly spilled the glass of water she was just setting down.

"Land sakes! Of course you'd wonder about THAT!" Dorothy went on to set the record straight.

Right. That's what I need. A bunch of old ladies calling themselves Happy Hookers clogging up the pathways, which are already nearly impossible to pass through.

"That's very kind of you, Dorothy, but I think Josh and I will need to tackle this by ourselves. And you saw the place—there's barely room for us, let alone extras. You could suggest some places that will accept some of that junk, however." While Dorothy pondered the possibilities, Katie said, "I told Josh maybe we should just hire a contractor to dig a big hole and shovel the whole place in it."

"Yes, he said you'd joked about that."

Joked? The idea is beginning to feel like the most inspired idea I've had in a long time.

"Well, Joshua was just a talking wonder during that drive, wasn't he?" Katie said with a bite in her voice.

"He's quite an interesting and expressive young man."

"Obviously he's been expressing more than you'd probably ever care to know."

"Goodness not. I'm always interested in what people have to say, especially young, energetic people, since they're gonna be running the country one day. I know you've got your plate pretty full right now, but should you need a break from your task and find you have a few spare moments, I'd love for you to drop by. There's something I'd like to talk to you about. I'm needing an informed outsider's opinion about a decision I need to make, and I have a feeling you're just the person who can help. In fact, I believe you might just be an answer to my prayers."

Katie wondered what in the world Dorothy was talking about, but she didn't have the energy to pursue it.

"Mom! You'll never guess what I just learned from Shelby. Dorothy, do you *really* have a computer? Are you *really* on-line?" Josh pulled out a chair and plunked himself down across from his mom next to Dorothy.

Josh leaned in toward Dorothy. Katie noticed how comfortable he'd become with her, how animated he became in her presence.

"Yup. And you might say I'm the fastest old lady in Partonville, since I just keep upgradin' away! I don't have enough time left in my life to spend it waiting for things to boot up and download! Would you like to see my office?"

"I sure would."

"Katie?"

"No, thank you. I think I'll just finish eating."

Dorothy and Josh bounded out of their chairs. No sooner were they out of sight than Gladys slipped into the chair across from Katie, who audibly sighed.

"It was a lovely service, dear. What did you think of Pastor Delbert's message?"

"It was fine." *And that's certainly all I'd share with you even if it weren't.*

"If, after you've been to your aunt's house, you need any assistance, please give the office a call. We'd be happy to help with any matters of business you might deem necessary."

"I have been to her house already, and I think we can manage just fine, thank you." Katie's tone of voice resonated assurance and finality.

That is, if we don't get talked to death first.

16

Guests long gone and things pretty well cleaned up, Dorothy went to check her e-mail.

Dear Dorothy, I didn't look at the piece of paper you wrote your e-mail address on until I got it out of my wallet when mom and I got back to the motel. I laughed out loud. "Outtamyway." Now that's a good one for you!

Mine's pretty boring compared to yours. Actually, I don't even like it anymore. I had to type something in when I set up the program several years ago, and it was the first thing that came to my mind. My best friend Alex Gillis started calling me that right after I met him when Mom and I moved into our brownstone. He lives next door. At this point, it just seems easier to keep it than change it. Besides, I haven't thought of a better one, so I'll just stick with Joshmeister.

Mom's taking a nap. We were going to go get boxes when we left the farm but when we got to the square, she said she'd changed her mind and we came straight here.

Thanks for sending me home with the brownies and pie. I already ate two of the brownies.

That's about it for now. I'll wait to see if I get an
answer before I write any more.

Josh.

Immediately Dorothy clicked on the "Reply to Sender"
icon and began typing away.

Dear Joshmeister, I think that name suits you just
fine! It sounds fun and important at the same time,
and by golly, we'd all do good to think of ourselves
that way!

I'm glad you enjoyed those brownies. I'll tell *my*
best friend, May Belle. (Of course, I'll have to phone
her. She wouldn't know which end of a computer to
plug in! Ha ha ha.) There's nothing she likes better
than to know her cooking has been appreciated,
and no one has appreciated her desserts over the
years more than me! It's a good thing you took some
of those brownies with you, or I'd have eaten them
all myself! Goodness knows you'd have to choke
down about anything I'd bake. Let's just say baking
isn't my gift.

I hope your mom gets a good nap. I imagine
you're both plenty tired.

Let me know if you need anything or if you'd just
like to come out to the farm to visit again. I could
show you the crooked creek our farm was named
after.

I try to check my e-mail at least twice a day when
I'm home. Of course, you can always phone, too. My
number is 555-7232.

Peace and grins, Dorothy.

After two more quick e-mailing volleys, since they were both on-line, Dorothy had learned, by reading not only Josh's words but between the lines, that he didn't have very many friends and that his best friend, Alex, didn't go to his school, that he didn't like the school he attended, that he used to play soccer in grade school but wasn't that good at it since he was kind of a slow runner, and that he didn't have a girlfriend. She'd also figured out that he longed for a better relationship with his mother. But then that one she'd figured out way before the e-mails.

When Katie and Josh pulled up in front of Aunt Tess's house at 3:00 P.M., they had to park behind The Tank. Giant stacks of boxes were piled on the front porch, and Earl was in the side yard using a hand sickle, continuing to tackle what he'd already accomplished in the front yard. Dorothy and May Belle were pulling weeds from the perennial flower garden along the sidewalk; Katie hadn't even noticed that flowers were growing there, the grass had been so tall.

"Oh, no," she groaned. "Look at all these people!"

"'Oh, yes' is what we should be saying, Mom. Look what a difference they've already made in this place. And no wonder Your Store was out of boxes!"

"I do not want these people nosing into our business, Joshua."

"I wouldn't say helping is nosing, Mom. Gads. Lighten up and appreciate the help for a change." He got out of the SUV and slammed the door.

Katie watched May Belle helping Dorothy up off her knees. Josh hurried over to support Dorothy's other arm.

She patted him on the cheek after she was upright, and he just beamed.

"There's a basket in the backyard, Josh." Dorothy pointed toward the open gateway in the fence. "Would you please put this big pile of weeds in it?" Earl didn't look up when Josh said "Howdy" as he passed by him on his way to carry out her request.

"Earl, honey, that'll do for now. We best be getting home and start dinner. We can finish later. Let's let Miss Katie begin her work in peace."

"Are you coming home with us, Dearest Dorothy?" Earl asked with hope in his eyes.

"Well, I reckon I could come by for a short visit. I bet I could even be talked into staying for dinner."

By this time Katie had approached them. "Won't you and Josh please join us, too?" May Belle asked expectantly. "We probably won't be eating until six, and that'll give you a chance to get a good bit of work done here. I just live around the corner."

"I expect we'll be working late tonight. Perhaps another time." Josh glared at her from the side yard, where he was stomping the overflow of weeds into the basket.

"I understand," May Belle replied. "You do what you need to do, dear."

"We'll be running along then, Katie," Dorothy said. "Let us know if you need more boxes."

"Thank you for getting these. That was kind of you." She heard Josh sigh. "And thank you for helping with the yard." Katie perused the tiny front yard, concluding that the clearing had, indeed, helped make it appear much less depressing.

"If there's anything else . . ." Dorothy's voice trailed off. She looked as though she was considering her next words.

"And please, if you'd like a break, like I said, I'd appreciate your opinions on an urgent issue. We could share a bite to eat, and Josh can do some exploring."

May Belle studied her friend's face. Dorothy's voice had sounded a bit tight when she talked about that urgent issue. Whatever it was, May Belle hoped it would settle itself soon, since it had obviously been weighing on Dorothy for some time now.

"Would you like a ride home, you two?" Dorothy asked May Belle and Earl.

"No. Goodness me, it's only a short hike, and the exercise will do us good, right, Earl?"

Earl gave a slight nod to his mom.

Josh came bounding around the side of the house. "Where's Sheba, Dorothy?"

"She was curled up on the end of my bed when I left home and barely opened one eye when I asked her if she wanted to go for a ride. I think all the excitement around there this morning just plumb wore her out."

Finally readied to enter the house and get to work, Katie stepped up to the front door and extracted the key from her handbag. She'd left it attached to its lace ribbon. The ladies waved good-bye as she turned the latch. Josh took the basket to the backyard. The last sound she heard before entering was the squealing of Dorothy's tires and gravel pelting the front of her Lexus. *You'd think I would have learned that lesson the last time I parked behind her!*

Dorothy finished putting the last of the dishes away. Although a few of the ladies from the church had stayed a bit after the funeral dinner to gather dirty dishes and help wash things up, she'd whipped into action gathering the boxes as soon as she'd finished with Josh's e-mails. She was glad to have her counters and kitchen table finally cleared off again. She could look at dust for days, maybe even weeks, but clutter drove her to distraction.

"There's no more avoiding it," she said to Sheba. "We've got to take a good study on those papers before Mr. Craig phones us again." She opened one of the little drawers, retrieved the key and unlocked the desk. She fixed herself a large ice water with lemon, then settled down at the kitchen table, holding the binder in her left hand while opening it with her right.

Lord, please let me understand what I'm looking at. Please. Help this old child of Yours be able to figure what's fair and what's not.

Make it clear to me what I should do. I just can't take this pondering any longer. And now, since I've been getting to know Josh, I just can't help but wonder what's the best thing for the youth in Partonville. Might they all leave before change comes? What will draw them back . . . or keep them here?

Just do something to make it clear. Amen from Dorothy.

After forty-five minutes of reading and rereading, Dorothy wasn't sure she knew any more than when she first began, other than that should she decide to sell the farm, she'd have more money than she needed or would ever live long enough to spend, and no doubt more than either of her sons or her grandkids *should* have after she was gone. She believed money could be the root of evil, were it not respected and at least partially labored for. She'd been raised with the notion that each generation should earn its own keep, especially when it came to land, or money garnered from it. She closed her eyes and rested her right hand across the pages.

Oh, Caroline Ann, daughter of mine, how different things would be if you had lived. You loved this place as much as I did. You surely did.

Dorothy pictured her daughter's gentle blue eyes the color of sky. The little mole on the side of her nose. The wisps of fine blond hair she was always pushing away from her face. Her prominent cheekbones shaped exactly like her daddy's.

"Oh, how I miss you." Upon hearing Dorothy's tone of voice, Sheba uncurled herself from the floor under the table and scratched at Dorothy's leg until she set the folder down and picked her up.

More than ten years had passed since Dorothy last cupped her daughter's sweet chin in her hands.

Caroline Ann Wetstra-Blankenship breathed her last breath at 1:20 A.M. on September 23, one of the first days of fall. She was a childless widow who lived thirty-nine years, six months and twelve days before succumbing to her third bout of cancer.

Caroline had waited thirty-two years to fall in love. When she did, marriage came fast and blissfully. Kenneth and Caroline both taught at the high school in Hethrow and met during a staff poetry reading. After a six-month, whirlwind courtship, their wedding date was announced. Kenneth was very happy to be moving to Crooked Creek with his new bride and Dorothy, who had quickly become one of his favorite people. Even though Dorothy protested that a new marriage didn't need an old mother living in it, she was outvoted and in truth thrilled that yet another generation would breathe life into Crooked Creek.

Even before the ceremony took place, Caroline and Kenneth fantasized about the "pack of wild ones" they'd one day have. Kenneth had been raised a city boy and found the land enchanting, quieting, healing almost. The afternoon Caroline rolled up her pant legs, took off her shoes and socks and splashed barefoot into the cool October waters of the creek to show him how to turn rocks and go crawdad huntin', he'd fallen in love with her all over again. He'd marched into the icy waters, gym shoes and all, just to kiss his giggling betrothed.

Their bountiful love was first pierced by illness, and then an automobile accident claimed Kenneth's life. Even though Caroline's faith in the God who loved her never waned, Dorothy sometimes wondered if the cancer didn't re-attack the fragments of Caroline's shattered heart before it bolted uncontrollably through her grief-stricken body.

When, at 11:00 P.M., the hospice nurse had made it clear Caroline would not make it through the night, Dorothy phoned in what she referred to as the "choir of angels to sing her home." Pastor, Nellie Ruth, May Belle and Dorothy circled around the hospital bed that for six weeks had been set up in the living room. For nearly two hours they sang hymns, stroked Caroline's arms, kissed her cheeks and lifted her in prayer. At 1:15 A.M. she opened her eyes and without moving her head deliberately smiled at each of them, ending with her mother. Although she soon closed her eyes, the smile remained on her lips.

Dorothy cupped her daughter's bony chin in her hands, looked full in her face, then gently settled her cheek against the sparse wisps of hair now left on her daughter's head. After a few moments of silence while Dorothy, eyes closed, felt the warmth of her daughter's faltering breath against her shoulder, Dorothy began to sing quietly the words she had sung to her precious daughter when Caroline was nursing at her breast. "Jesus loves you, this I know . . ." She didn't stop singing until Pastor stepped behind Dorothy, put a hand on each of her shoulders and whispered, "It is finished, Dorothy. She's standing in front of Jesus now. He's scooping her into His arms and welcoming her home."

Tears streamed down Dorothy's face and onto page three of the document before her as she leaned over the table, cradling Sheba tightly in her arms. Sheba maneuvered until she could put one tentative paw on Dorothy's chest, then began licking away her salty tears.

"Sheba, you sure would have liked my Caroline! For someone who had one of the roughest lives imaginable, she just kept on loving the Lord. Said she couldn't imagine how people got through trials without Him. And trials she had." Sheba settled back down into Dorothy's lap. Dorothy took several long drinks of water as though trying to quench her thirst for her own flesh and blood while washing down her grief.

17

The rumble of thunder in the west prompted Katie and Josh to haul the boxes inside. After thoroughly surveying things, it was determined the only place to put them was in the kitchen near the back door, where they stacked them as high as they could go. She hated to crowd the only place in the house where she felt she had room to take a deep breath, but there was no other choice.

She and Josh smooshed together in the hallway and decided that was where they had to begin the overwhelming task before them. They'd work their way toward the living room after clearing the hall. Aunt Tess's bedroom would come next and the little back bedroom last. From what she could recall when she'd peeked in there the other day, that back room appeared to be mostly piles of furniture stacked to the ceiling.

"Mom, have we got a flashlight in the Lexus?"

"Of course. In the emergency box I keep in the back. Why?"

"I thought I'd tape one to my head. Since we're acting like coal miners, I might as well look like one." He shot her a devilish grin.

"Josh, get the two largest boxes and line them up in front of the stove. Look in the kitchen drawers, and if by some miracle you can find a felt marker, label the boxes 'Garbage' and 'Giveaway.' If you can't find a marker, let's have a rule that the garbage box is always on the left and the giveaway is on the right."

"Where will we put stuff we want to keep?"

"In one of those two boxes, Joshua. The last thing we need is any of *this* junk."

Josh started rummaging through drawers and was surprised to find them as neat as the rest of the kitchen. Not only did he find a marker, he also found a box of heavy-duty black plastic garbage bags.

"Score! I got a better idea, Mom. Let's make both boxes giveaway, and we can each drag a garbage bag around with us so we don't have to keep walking to the kitchen with everything."

"Why, Joshua Matthew Kinney, that is brilliant!"

"Really?" His eyebrows flew up in the air as if they'd been launched, and his eyes lit up.

"Don't let it go to your head."

"Right." He noticed his mom had picked fresh flowers and filled the vase on the table. It was still set exactly as it had been when they arrived, place mats, unlit candle, water glasses and all. He'd caught his mom staring at the photo more than once. And no doubt about it, the silo in that photo was Dorothy's.

Although Katie hated thinking about the possibility that anyone would come peer in the windows, it was shortly concluded that there wasn't enough light in the hallway to accomplish much of anything. She had Josh crawl over piles of things on the couch in the living room to reach the blinds on the side windows and throw them open, then stand on the bed in the bedroom to roll up the shades, at least allowing a slight bit more light to penetrate the work area. That it was cloudy outside didn't help the cause, and soon it would be dark.

"Okay, I'll start left and you go right, Josh. Let's clear the whole hall so we can get through to the kitchen when we start the other rooms."

"How will I know what's garbage and what's worth giving away?"

"If you don't know what it is or if it's broken or ripped, chuck it. We simply will never get through if we allow ourselves to begin evaluating."

"What about papers like bills and things?"

Katie sighed and thought about the question. "We'll have to start another box, I guess. Let's put any documents and correspondence in it. I can go through that later. Of course, throw newspapers and magazines and junk mail away. Keep a sharp eye out for Aunt Tess's trust papers. No doubt we'll need them one day soon."

"Mom, I wonder if they recycle here in Pardon Me Ville. Since I found out Ms. Outtamyway has a computer, who knows what else we might expect?"

"Miss who?"

"Dorothy. That's her Internet name."

"That certainly fits her."

Josh watched his mom stuff a pile of junk mail, a hairbrush, four bottles of fingernail polish and an empty coffee-filter box into her plastic bag. He concluded that, much to his surprise, his mom obviously wasn't interested in recycling even if Partonville had it. She was the one who usually hauled his pop cans and fast-food Styrofoam containers out of the trash at home, lecturing all the while. He knew better than to bring that up now, however, and decided to just follow her lead. And so the dig-out process began.

The hallway seemed to be packed mostly with personal items of clothing, years' worth of the *Partonville Press* and toiletries that didn't make their way back to the bathroom, which was the second neatest room in the house. *Thank goodness!* Katie had exclaimed when she saw it.

Katie had never seen so much polyester in her life. There were pantsuits of nearly every color folded one on top of the other. Obviously Aunt Tess hadn't been clothes shopping for decades. She picked them up by the armloads and tossed them in one of the giveaway boxes. Garbage bag after garbage bag was quickly filled, mostly with newspapers and flyers. Josh tied them with twist ties, then took them out on the back stoop, where it was now softly sprinkling and the faint rumbles of thunder were all but gone, the storm having missed Partonville.

Three large giveaway boxes were quickly topped off. Josh was stunned when his mom tossed him the keys and asked him to back the Lexus around to the gate. This was only the second time he'd ever been behind the wheel of the Cashmere Beige LX470. Katie had purchased it as a reward to herself after her last big development deal. She had boldly aced nemesis Keith Benton out of a six-hundred-acre parcel prime for the shopping center, school and housing development that now graced Kane County. Although she'd enjoyed the Mercedes SL500, it no longer packed the punch of "this mother of SUVs," as Josh liked to refer to it.

Ever so slowly and carefully, he backed up to the opening, getting out twice to see how much room was left before he'd hit the gateposts. He folded both rows of backseats to the sides and started packing in the boxes, pushing them way to the front. Then he loped back into the kitchen to do some reorganizing.

Katie came into the kitchen to retrieve a drink of water just as he was whamming the bottom of the box containing documents and mail. He'd dumped it into a bigger box, since he'd way underestimated the size box this would take. She groaned and mumbled something about probably not living long enough to sort through the "mountains of mayhem."

"'Mountains of mayhem'? That's a new one! Where'd ya get that?"

Katie stopped in her tracks for a moment to think. Where had she gotten that one? It seemed just to spring out of her mouth without her thinking about it. "Mountains of mayhem. Mountains of mayhem." She repeated it aloud like a mantra while she zoomed through her memory bank. "I have no earthly idea," she stated flatly, then she began picking through the papers, reading return addresses and postmarks aloud. "'Pierce Hospital, May 2, 1974.' 'Richardson's Rexall Drugs, December 12, 1998.' Gads." She blew loudly through her mouth, tossed them back in the box and went back to work.

The first time Katie looked at her watch it was 7:30 P.M. No sooner had she lifted her head from reading the dial than there was a loud pounding on the door, nearly scaring her out of her wits!

"Who in the world . . ." She made her way through the path in the living room to the front door, which had no window or peephole. Cautiously she opened the door. There stood the last man she either expected or wanted to see—none other than the rude man who had locked them out of Harry's Grill. He was still wearing his food-smeared apron. They stood there glaring at one another for a moment, then he spoke.

"Katie Durbin?"

"Yes." Katie set her jaw.

"Lester K. Biggs. Word around town is that you need boxes. I got a shipment of canned and boxed goods today. Usually I cut them up right away, but seeing as how there's a need, I just slit the tops and brung 'em over. I'll just leave 'em here by the door if that's all right with you." Without waiting for a response, he turned on his heels and headed for his pickup, retrieving two boxes, which he stacked right in front of her.

"That's it. Need more?"

"Probably."

"Fine. I'll drop them off as I get them." He whirled around, went back to his truck, opened the front door, reached across the front seat and strode up to Katie again, this time with a large white paper sack folded down at the top. "Brought you the rest of today's stew. Figure you had silverware." He thrust the bag at her, which she grabbed with her right hand. Again he whirled and went to his truck, only to return once more, this time carrying a jar.

"Here. I took a small collection at my place for anyone who didn't send flowers but who might wanna give a little something toward . . . whatever." He glanced at the front of her showy Lexus, which stuck out from beside the house, then back at her again. "Probably don't need this, but folks around here are generous no matter what."

Katie accepted the Miracle Whip jar. It was filled with coins and a couple of bills.

"I been good and bawled out by more than one customer. Didn't mean to be rude to you the other day. Nothin' personal. Closin' time is closin' time."

Whirl. In truck. Gone.

Mouth agape. Eat. Call it a day.

It was late Saturday evening when Josh retrieved his e-mail back at the Lamp Post. Josh popped open the lid to a can of Pepsi, set it down on the desk next to him and logged on. He was glad to learn he had two messages waiting.

> Dear Joshmeister. Tell your mom not to haul your discards to Now and Again Resale. I've got a better idea, and it's a dandy. We'll stop by after church tomorrow to tell you about it. Of course you're both welcome to attend services with us at 10:00 a.m. if you like. Dorothy and Sheba, Queen of the Mutt Dogs.

> Joshmeister! I'm glad to hear things are getting done. Well, maybe done isn't the right word but you know what I mean. I wish I could see that house. Are you sure you're not exaggerating? Any more news about that blonde baseball player you met? Melany dumped me. That's okay. She was pretty boring anyway. Mom's calling me. I didn't take out the garbage. As you can tell, nothing has changed here since you've been gone, including me. Alex.

Dorothy pulled up in front of Aunt Tess's on her way home from church Sunday, just when Katie and Josh were re-arranging the back of the Lexus, filling the last possible square inch. Sheba came bounding up to Josh, who happily picked her up and nuzzled her with his nose.

"Well, howdy do," Dorothy said with enthusiasm. "Looks like you two have been busier than two gnats on a bunch of old bananas."

"Boy, am I glad to see you, Dorothy. Mom's nearly worked my fingers to the bone."

Katie shot a quizzical look at her son, who had not complained once about their labors. Josh had, in fact, even seemed to enjoy himself while they were working, once putting a felt hat with orange feathers on his head and prancing around like a ballerina, causing Katie to laugh out loud. She learned more about events at his school than she'd ever heard him share before. He asked her probing questions about her childhood, and she found herself reminiscing about things she didn't even know she remembered. His statement to Dorothy felt oddly wounding to Katie. In fact, aside from the hard physical labor, things had been going reasonably well. May Belle stopped by once with a pot of chicken and noodles and another time with a Tupperware bowl filled with warm chocolate chip cookies. Boxes showed up on the doorstep at all hours of the day, just when they needed them. . . .

"Well," Dorothy responded, ignoring Josh's obvious teasing quip to his mother, "when there's much to be done, the best thing to do is, just do it!" Dorothy said, sounding like the Nike commercial.

"Actually, your timing is perfect. As you can see," Katie said, making a grand sweeping gesture with her arm, "we've just packed the Lexus to the gills, and I'm needing to make a run so we can load up again. What's the idea you e-mailed Josh about?"

"I can give you something even better to do with those things than haul them all the way to Yorkville, dear. I talked with the Social Concerns Committee at church this morning, and they all agreed we'd be honored to accept your donations for our fall rummage sale. As usual, I'm collecting and pricing things in my barn as they come in, with the help of the rest of the committee, of course. All the funds we raise from this event go to our Mission Support Committee. And, well," she said hesitantly, breaking eye contact, "there might just be an auction coming up, too."

"Auction? Cool. I've never been to an auction before!" Josh exclaimed. "Where and when is *that*? I hope we're still around."

Dorothy noticed movement on the neighbor's front porch. Sorry she'd mentioned it at all, and certainly not wanting to open this can of worms where a Partonville resident could get wind of it, she backpedaled a bit, saying it was all too uncertain to count on but assuring them that the rummage sale would definitely take place.

"I don't know what a mission support committee is," Katie said, "but if they're willing to accept all this stuff, they can certainly have it."

"Seeing as it's lunchtime, how about you and Josh just follow me out to the farm and have a bite with me. I've still got a mess of ham and potatoes left over from the funeral. It'll just take a minute to zap 'em."

Josh grinned at the surprising blend of old and new he continued to discover about this feisty woman. "Excellent idea, Dorothy!" he exclaimed as he slammed the back door to the Lexus closed.

Katie looked thoughtful for a moment, then agreed. "Actually, I could use a breath of fresh air myself." Josh looked surprised but beamed at his mother's response. "Go on ahead, Dorothy. We'll make sure things are locked up here, then we'll be right out."

"I imagine Outtamyway will travel faster than we can keep up with anyway." Josh looked first at his mom, then turned his head and winked at Dorothy, who laughed.

"Well, I have been accused of having a lead foot on more than one occasion, I confess. At my age, however, there's no time to waste. Like the Good Book says, my days are numbered. At eighty-seven, I imagine I'm down to my numbered breaths. I don't have time to waste going slow!

"Come on, Sheba. Time to hit the road. We've got company a-comin'."

18

Dorothy was standing by the barn when Katie and Josh arrived. She was acting like a flagman on an aircraft carrier, laughing at her own gyrations when Josh stuck his arms and head out the car window and began pretending to be signaling her back. Although Katie's breath hitched a bit at the sight of the silo, she found the tall structure had now become oddly comforting, since she'd spent so much time gazing at it in that photo on Aunt Tess's table.

Dorothy had Josh slide open the massive barn doors, which, as of the last few years and much to her disgruntlement, were more than she could manage alone anymore. Perhaps that was yet another reason to consider selling: get out before she and the place both just fell apart or Challie Carter got too old or disinclined to lease her land to farm. Under Dorothy's direction, Katie backed the Lexus right up into the loft. Josh and Katie finished unloading the boxes, stacking them next to two long banquet tables piled with miscellaneous items ranging from toasters to curling irons to old Avon bottles, which were covered with sheets of clear plastic to protect them from the elements. Dorothy said she'd be renting more tables when the time came and that their multiple deposits would be fine just stacked in place.

Josh took notice of his surroundings. The barn smelled

of hay and earth. Never in his life had he inhaled anything so heavenly. Slices of sunlight beamed in through cracks in the slatted barn walls, and dust particles danced in their light. A couple of pigeons darted from one beam to another, giving life to the stillness. The floorboards were worn by decades of tractor wheels, and a frayed rope hung from a beam. He just stood, staring, listening, inhaling deeply, taking it all in.

Dorothy noticed Josh reveling in his senses, then looked at Katie, who herself seemed to be mesmerized. Dorothy walked past them and slid open the four-by-six-foot side door, revealing a topside view of the stunning breadth of Crooked Creek Farm. She, too, drew a deep breath and leaned against the doorframe, dangling her right leg out over the ledge.

"I have lived here for eighty-seven years and never tired of this beauty. I must say, I had my fair share of travels when I was conducting and we were in competitions across the country. But nothing has captured me like this view from my own barn door."

Katie moved beside Dorothy and studied the look of peace on her face, trying to remember the last time she'd viewed something that spoke to her the way this land obviously did to Dorothy—the last time she'd felt that seemingly peaceful about *anything*. Slowly Katie panned from right to left, drinking in the vista.

Yes, there *was* something about this place. Yes.

Josh, Katie and Dorothy shared a lovely afternoon together, swapping stories, as Dorothy called it, eating leftovers and then meandering down by the creek. Dorothy said it wasn't fitting that a boy Josh's age hadn't learned how to hunt crawdads, and today was as good a day as any.

The crooked creek for which the farm was named wound its way through the property about a quarter mile back of the barn, just on the other side of the willow trees and an old cottonwood. Dorothy pointed to the trees as they passed, one after the other, referring to them as though they were people. "Meet Weeping Willy, Woodsy, Willoway . . ." Dorothy turned to face Katie and noticed her jaw had dropped. "Do you know each tree has its own personality?" Dorothy didn't wait for a response. "They display it in their leaves and bark and the stories they collect. Why, Woodsy houses the imprints of hundreds of toes that have climbed those powerful branches just to get high enough over the creek to jump in."

She led them around Woodsy to what had always been referred to as the swimmin' hole, a portion of the creek that was deeper than the rest, carved by years of water rushing around the hairpin turn. Although it wasn't quite warm enough for swimmin', Dorothy assured Josh that if she wasn't too old to crawdad hunt, neither was he. With that statement out of her mouth, she began to untie her white tennis shoes, peel back her pink socks and roll up her pant legs. Josh followed suit. When they both were barefoot and wiggling their toes, she then placed her hands on her cocked hip, looked straight at Katie and asked her what *she* was waiting for.

"I guess I'm just not the crawdad type," she said, tucking a flyaway hair behind her ear.

Dorothy considered whether to challenge her, then decided she'd best not, since she was soon going to be counting on her alliance and didn't want to do anything to alienate the hand she hoped would help guide her.

"Well, it's you and me, Joshmeister! Just do what I do and keep your eyes open." With that, she stepped into the foot-deep cool waters just north of the swimmin' hole, bent nearly in half until her face was as close to the rushing waters as her five-foot, ten-inch frame would allow, and began to stare. Remaining folded in half, she took a couple splashing steps and stared again. At the first sign of a sizable rock, she slowly sank her hand into the waters and gently picked up the edge with one hand, poising the other nearby. Like a flash, a crawdad seemed to squirt out amid the cloud of mud that swirled into the water from beneath the rock. Just as quickly, Dorothy stabbed her free hand into the waters and picked him up by the tail, waving the four-inch squirmer in the air and grinning from ear to ear.

"Now that's how it's done. Your turn."

Josh laughed out loud, then gave a loud war hoop and beat himself on the chest a couple times. "Mighty hunter go for game," he said in a guttural tone. After three tries, he, too, had his first catch of the day. Katie stood on the bank watching Dorothy's face transform into that of a twelve-year-old. No doubt about it, Dorothy Wetstra was a sight to behold.

By the time they sauntered their way back up to the farmhouse, it was late afternoon. Although Katie had forgotten Dorothy's curious statement about needing opinions and her being an answer to prayer, Dorothy certainly had not.

She was afraid if she didn't just jump right into the subject when they entered the kitchen, her courage and the opportunity would slip away. Time was running out . . . for a lot of things.

"Katie, I need to talk to you about something of dire importance. I have spent too long fretting and praying over a big decision in my life, and like I said before, I believe God has, as usual and in His perfect timing, and in the nick of time, I might add"—she looked skyward when she said those words—"provided just what I need, and that would be you. I have to trust someone."

Katie drew a deep breath and held it for a moment as she studied the look of determination that etched itself onto Dorothy's face. Long gone was the youthful exuberance inspired by bare feet and crawdads. The face she saw before her now exuded weariness, possibly even pain.

Although Josh's curiosity was piqued, he had the distinct feeling it would be better if he left them alone. After getting Dorothy's permission to crank up her computer and log on to AOL, he headed upstairs to her office.

"Please, dear, sit down," Dorothy said. Katie pulled up a chair at the kitchen table across from her and leaned on her forearms.

"Sit tight a minute," Dorothy said. "I've got to get something. And would you like a glass of water while we're chatting? I need to wet my whistle. All that walking plumb dried up my spit!"

"Yes, that would be nice." Katie studied her chipped nail polish and pondered how all the unaccustomed manual labor was taking its toll on her all-togetherness. Her hands were dry and chafed from relentless washing as she tried to keep herself at least somewhat sanitized from the years of Aunt Tess's neglect. Dorothy zipped from here to there, finally returning with two waters with lemon and a large folder she plunked down on the table between them.

"Craig & Craig Developers?" Katie was shocked, the look on her face revealing one of recognition. *Those are the guys Keith Benton invests with in this part of the country!*

"Yes, have you heard of them?"

"Of course. In fact, I've come up against them a few times."

"Come up against them?"

"Not exactly directly and not in the bad sense of the word. Just business dealings. You could say I've won a few rounds, and they've won a few more," Katie said, recalling her last losing volley with disgust. The one the Lexus still hadn't made up for.

"Well, I need to trust you, Katie. You see," she said, pausing a moment to take a deliberate couple gulps of water while she silently prayed God would help her gather her courage and thoughts in a manner that would come out right, "I am an old lady. That is obvious. And although I was born and raised on Crooked Creek Farm, and Henry and I raised three children on this spread, and lots of others have partied and healed here, there is no one in my family who wants it when I'm gone. Oh, Caroline Ann had the same heart for this place as myself, but it wasn't in God's plans for her to have it."

"Caroline Ann?"

"My daughter. My beautiful daughter."

"Where is she?"

Dorothy said the next words so quietly that it took Katie a moment to digest them. "With Jesus."

"I am so sorry. How long has she . . ."

"She died over ten years ago. She was only thirty-nine years old. She and her husband moved right in with me after their wedding. Can you imagine them wanting to do such a thing?"

Katie thought about how different this usually joyful and somewhat wild woman was from *her* mother. There always seemed to be an indefinable sadness lurking inside her mom. Although Katie'd loved her mom, no, she certainly could not imagine trying to live with her, since they were so different.

Dorothy didn't wait for an answer; she just charged right on in a near blur of words. "I have two sons. Jacob Henry is my oldest. He, like many younguns these days, couldn't wait to get out of Partonville when he got old enough to go to college. He went to Penn State and never looked back. Oh, of course he comes home for visits. He just doesn't stay long when he does. He gets antsy and impatient after a few days and usually finds a reason to leave before he originally intended.

"Now, don't misunderstand. I love that firstborn child of mine, just the way he is. I simply don't kid myself about reality." She chuckled. "In fact, he reminds me a bit of you. So much to do. So serious."

Katie wasn't sure how to take that comment. Again, Dorothy continued right on before she could file the remark.

"He never married. Came close a couple times but seemed to find something wrong with each of them just when everyone thought he'd be popping the question. He's a lawyer in Philadelphia. Mostly represents big business. He's as happy as he can manage to be, I imagine, although I do keep asking Jesus to soften him a bit.

"Partonville has begun to suffer the last many years from all the kiddos who've moved away. A town needs youth, energy, new ideas, or else it becomes stale and crotchety. Unless a child wants to farm, there's not been much around for them, other than the mines. They go out and find the rest of the world and then . . ." She was silent for a moment. "A few businesses on the square have already closed. Can't help but wonder how long some others can hang on.

"I used to think my other son, Vincent, might end up living here. After his baby sister died, he stayed here with me a couple weeks. I'd watch him disappear down toward the creek, shoulders shaking as he sobbed. He didn't want to keep falling apart in front of me." She sat quietly for a moment, refolding her hands. "He has always been so tenderhearted. It liked to kill him when Joan, his ex-wife, took Bradley and Steven and left him. Those towheaded kids are young teenagers now! They were just little guys when they came for a couple days to stay with their dad during our grieving. I'd watch Vinnie watching those kids, realizing they never had a chance to run free and wild like this, what with all the worries in the city. Oh, how Vinnie used to run like the wind through those fields!

"But it wasn't meant to be for those youngsters either. He met Joan at Southern Illinois University when they were juniors. She was from Denver, and she wanted to be near her folks after graduation. Vinnie found a solid banking job, and off they went. He maintains a very close relationship with his sons since the divorce, and he'd never move away from them. He's got him a right swell girlfriend, and they've been dating about two years now, but I think he's still working himself to the place where he can trust a woman. I pray every day for his healing to be complete so he can get on with his life and not end up alone." Her voice sounded weak at the end of her statement, and she drifted off into her own thoughts for a moment.

Katie couldn't help but notice that it appeared this spunky lady was literally shrinking on the spot. Her normal bolt-upright posture had begun rounding off in the last few minutes, as though she were melting from the weight of hard memories.

Katie studied each line in Dorothy's face. *I can't believe all of what I've heard! She's always so upbeat and funny. So spunky and ready to help. How does she manage to be so positive after having lost a daughter and been all but abandoned by her sons? How old did she say Caroline was when she died? Gads, she was younger than I am!*

Dorothy shook her head and bolted out of her chair, startling Katie. She zipped into the dining room, opened the treasured mahogany desk and pulled out a photo album, returning to the table with it. She stood next to Katie and flipped through the pages, landing on the one she was seeking, and handed the entire album over, opened to the spot.

"See? These are my children." Her arthritic finger moved and pointed at the speaking of each name. "Jacob Henry, Vincent and Caroline Ann. We had the boys so close together, they were raised more like twins. Then Caroline Ann didn't come along till quite some time later. This here is my faithful Henry. Of course, that's me."

Katie felt a rush of warmth as she perused their faces. The similarities from nose to chin to eyes filtered throughout their strong bloodline. The way they stood so close together, husband to wife and sibling to sibling. . . . Dorothy leaned in and flipped the pages again.

"Here's Vinnie with his younguns. That one there is Steven. That devilish little booger is Bradley. He'll give you a run for your money, that's for sure!" It didn't go unnoticed by Katie that the lilt was back in Dorothy's voice. "Here's Caroline Ann and Jacob the year before she died. The boys were home for Thanksgiving, too, when I snapped these." Nearly all the pictures were taken outside, different angles of the house and land framing the faces.

Katie couldn't stop staring at the photos. So drawn into the life of this woman was she that there was nearly a tug of war over the album when Dorothy said they could finish looking at it another time but that now they needed to talk business.

Katie leaned her head back against the tub and scootched down until her entire body was cocooned in the steaming water topped with bubbles that peaked like oceans of whipped cream. Closing her eyes, she tried to draw a blank, release the turmoil that had captured her earlier in the day when Dorothy entrusted her with such startling information. The swarm of thoughts, however, simply would not sink, no matter how deeply she submerged into the waters.

Craig & Craig's proposal was for the entire Crooked Creek Farm—160 acres. Dorothy seemed to think the price they were offering per acre was "gracious." Katie ran the figures in her head. Although it was more, she speculated, than most local farmers would probably be able to pay, were Dorothy to pursue *that* avenue, by no stretch of the imagination were they being "gracious"—even with the risks of such a purchase.

She did, however, understand Craig & Craig's chop licking. The lure of sweet revenge swelled within her.

Katie raced the Lexus past Dorothy's to the contingent edge of Hethrow the next morning and spent a good couple of hours poking around, also making prying phone calls without tipping her base of information or the true reason for her inquiries. Should word spread about a prime-location landholder's possible interest in selling that many acres, other commercial offers would undoubtedly spring to life and drive up the price per acre, perhaps even as much as double it. In fact, she imagined even without word spreading, other deals were ready to hit the table; there was just too much going on in Hethrow for there not to be. She spent a good while in the courthouse and library gleaning whatever she could, prowling around on the Internet as well. Luckily Hethrow was the county seat, and public information was plentiful.

She pondered the possibilities, trying to predict Craig & Craig's plans for residential development. *Yes, that's probably what it would be. Undoubtedly they could at least sell two lots per acre, maybe even three. There was already a trend set on that end of Hethrow toward mid- to upper-range homes starting at $175,000, easily topping the quarter-million or more mark. It looks like there could also be a need for new schools, should all Crooked Creek land become residential. Those Landers people next door would then become the next likely contingent target. Whew! Those prices would be through the ceiling! And surely the Craigs have an inside pulse* *of Hethrow's city planners' intentions to allow for more annexation, or they wouldn't be going after such a score.* She wondered how those in charge of Partonville might receive the challenge, but knew one day they'd have to, and probably soon.

She was alive with the hunt, captured by the opportunity and haunted by the trust of Dorothy Jean Wetstra.

19

Dear Outtamyway,

Alex says to tell you Hello. He thinks you must be one of the coolest old ladies ever. He couldn't believe I'd been crawdad hunting and that you were the one who taught me how. In fact, he didn't even know what a crawdad was until I explained it looked something like a miniature lobster but brown instead of red.

I hope you don't mind me using the term old lady. I mean, you are old. But you don't seem like it. In fact, you seem "younger" than my mom, if you know what I mean.

Speaking of mom, she's been gone all morning. I got to sleep in for a change. She slid a note under my door saying she was going to run some errands, and I didn't find it until I woke up at 9:20. Usually she's banging on my door at 7:30 or so. She said she hoped to be back at noon. She promised me yesterday that we'd have lunch today at Harry's. Can you believe it?!

Hope to see you soon. Joshmeister.

Dear Joshmeister,

I am an old lady, and that's a fact. No sense acting any other way.

Tell Alex he must be cool, too, since he's your best friend.

I'm glad you got to sleep in. I guess that hunting expedition wore you out. HA! I slept in a little myself this morning, but then Sheba and I stayed up late watching an old Joan Crawford movie on TV. I don't imagine you know who she is. I ate microwave popcorn, and I do believe there's still some kernels stuck in my upper plate.

Have fun at Harry's. I had breakfast there this morning. You'll likely meet some real characters. Oh, and you might want to wear a helmet (that ought to get you wondering ;>). Hope to see you soon. XO

Dorothy recalled her wild breakfast at Harry's that morning. Folks had been buzzing like berserk bees about Harold's provocative editorial in Sunday's *Partonville Press,* "Riding the Fence of Development." Since the grill was always closed on Sunday, Monday morning was the first chance they'd had to let their emotions run rampant, aside from church, which just wouldn't have been appropriate. Words had been flying so quickly, Dorothy nearly felt that she had to duck to keep from getting pelted with them. It was as close to chaos as she'd ever witnessed, what with heads bobbing up and down, people leaning across each other to get something repeated, shouting across the U. . . .

She'd overheard bits and pieces of Lester's coffee-pouring

talk, rambling on about a red Toyota he'd heard tell about. Gladys held court, blustering something about an interview Sharon had apparently had with Colton Craig. "Over my dead body will they. . . . ," she ranted, once even banging the counter. Arthur hollered at Lester, "Quit actin' like a girlie gossip and git my eggs a-cookin'!" Cora Davis didn't park her backside in her chair once, she was so busy flitting from person to person, passing around what she heard from each set of lips. Even Challie Carter showed up to see how folks were speculating after that editorial. He wondered if this might not be the time to stop farming all that leased land, sell *his* entire estate lock, stock and barrel, and head for retirement in Florida: "Trade in my coveralls for one of those shirts with palm trees on it."

Harold and Dorothy had been the only two who sat quietly, listening to the cacophony. She was afraid to jump into the conversation, since she was such a bad liar and something might show on her face. She occasionally nodded her head, just to let them know she was "in" on the dialogue. Of course, Dorothy was the *last* person they'd imagine was talking to someone, literally holding them all on the verge of Change with a capital *C,* and that meant progress—or did it? She wondered, if she did accept the Craigs' offer and the sale went through, what might they think of her then. Although all the development talk certainly caused her breath to hitch, she'd finally relaxed a bit, learning at least that Mr. Craig was indeed a man of his word and hadn't said anything.

Harold had studied Dorothy. Just kept tapping his pen on the counter and looking her way, seemingly drawn into her . . . silence. It caused her pretty much to gobble down her breakfast and retreat back home.

The one thing she knew for sure was that eventually progress would march its way into Partonville. For better or for worse—and she usually came down on the side of modernization—progress would come, and perhaps her last hurrah on this earth could be that of opening the door to it.

Partonville had shrunk a bit over the last decade, and she'd rather see it have to change than disappear completely. She couldn't stand to imagine what would happen to her farm if she didn't take some kind of steps. Why, what if she died without making any decisions? What would happen to her land then? No, better to take action rather than just let things happen. She hadn't been raised to be passive. Her dad would likely roll over in his grave if he thought for a moment she hadn't made some kind of plans for Crooked Creek upon her death!

Last evening, Katie had even given her hope there might be a very special way to preserve the memories of the Crooked Creek Farm for her children and her children's children, even if she were to sell it. Colton Craig had given her no idea she held the power to call a few shots. For instance, Katie said she could include in the deal that a certain number of acres be donated to the conservation district. *Crooked Creek Park. Now how would that sit with you, Mom, Dad, Henry, Caroline Ann? Think the angels would dance to the likes of that?* Or would they weep? Well, that was the one thing she could be assured wouldn't happen, since there were no tears in heaven.

Dorothy also knew progress at Aunt Tess's had been speedier than anyone expected and that Katie was eager to get Josh back in school and get herself back to the grind, as she referred to it, although any time she mentioned going home, Dorothy noticed Josh's face dull a bit. It had not gone unnoticed by Dorothy that that boy longed for his mother's attention, and somehow this trip seemed to be softening her edges. At the very least it had opened doors of communication she knew had been closed. Josh had revealed more to her in his ongoing e-mails than even he might have imagined—that he felt like an oddball in his own school and felt more at home in Partonville, that he seemed more curious about his grandmother's past than his mother did about her own mother.

Dorothy also knew she'd grown very fond of Joshmeister and, in fact, found herself praying for him nightly, along with his mother.

When Josh and Katie entered Harry's at twelve-thirty, heads snapped and tongues stopped wagging. Even though most of the folks had departed, including the early lunch crowd, and conversations had worn down, Partonvillers didn't believe in airing their laundry to strangers. Cora Davis had already come and gone—no doubt working her way from store to store and telephone line to telephone line—so Katie and Josh parked themselves at her usual table at the window.

"Dorothy was here for breakfast, Mom. Too bad we didn't come earlier! She said we might need helmets today, but I don't see anything different than we ever have. I don't know what she was talking about. At least sitting here we won't miss any of the action. We can be the Shift Two Gawkers," he said, then laughed.

"Joshua! Keep your voice down. It's bad enough I'm actually going to be subjected to all this grease," she said as she looked at the menu, "without also being shunned in the process. And how do you know Dorothy was here for breakfast? Did she phone you this morning?"

"No, we e-mailed back and forth a few times."

"E-mail? Already this morning?"

"Yes. I told you that."

"Well, I hope you . . ."–she paused for a moment to weigh her words–"know where the boundaries of friendship and private affairs begin and end."

"Oh, yes, ma'am," he said with sarcasm, then gave her a crisp salute. "How can you worry so much and talk that way about . . ."–he used his fingers to air-play quotation marks "'these people'? They've done nothing but help. Mom, even Lester Biggs has gone out of his way to bring us all the boxes and food and . . ."

"What do you want to order?" The question came without warning and with no softness around the edges. Lester spat it out before he even arrived tableside.

"Hi, Mr. Biggs. We sure appreciate all you've done for us," Josh chirped.

Lester nodded acknowledgment of the statement, then lifted his order pad.

"Do you have a special today, Mr. Biggs?" Josh asked, unaffected by Lester's curtness.

Lester didn't speak but pointed his pencil at the three-by-five index card sandwiched between the salt and paper shakers. Josh fingered the card and read it out loud to his mom. "BLT with noodle soup plus pie and coffee. I'll have that, sir," Josh said.

"Make it two," Katie added, "but keep my dessert. And do you have decaf?"

"Course," he kind of grunted, as though she was daft. Josh volunteered to eat his mom's dessert, too, and asked for a Coke rather than coffee. Lester made notations on his notepad and silently returned to the grill, collecting a couple empty coffee cups from the counter on his way.

The screen door slammed so loudly that Katie yelped aloud. Earl was returning with the empty delivery box from today's late lunchtime round.

Josh finished off the last scrap of piecrust on his second dessert. "So what was up with Dorothy yesterday? What was so important she had to talk to you?" he asked, licking the fork between words, making the *you* sound as though it astonished him.

Katie heard the squeak of stools and noticed two customers had turned to face them. "For goodness sake, lower your voice, Joshua. It wasn't anything, really." Josh noticed she didn't make eye contact with him when she answered, nor did he believe her. His mom had been wired ever since they'd left Dorothy's yesterday. She'd also evaded answering his questions as to her whereabouts all morning, muttering something he couldn't understand, then changing the subject.

Dorothy was glad she'd had Josh leave the barn doors open a crack so she could wiggle in. She stood in her favorite place in her girlish pose, foot dangling over the ledge, looking out over the farmlands.

"Dear Lord," she said aloud, causing a couple of pigeons to shift beams in the cool, dark, cavernous space. "It's me, Dorothy Jean, but then I reckon You already know that." She paused for a moment and gazed up toward the sky as though centering her attention. "I know I've been a downright pest the last week or so, but since You know everything, You already know Mr. Craig has phoned me again. He reminded me the contract offer expires in two days and that he'd like to have an official answer rather than just letting it expire. Me, too. I don't mean I'd like to expire, but that I'd like to have an answer, too. Now, although I know You want me to have patience, I have plumb run out. The weight of this decision is more than I can take. Please! Do something! Make it clear. I'm listening. Amen."

She turned to walk away from the door, then whirled back around.

"Wait! I don't know what's gonna become of this place, but it occurs to me I also don't know where I'll go if I do move. And I'm not talking about heaven yet! Be working on that, too, if You decide I'm outtahere. Okay? And give me strength and courage for . . . whatever. Whatever. Isn't that a great word, Lord? You can end just about every sentence with it. Amen again. And I mean it this time."

Katie and Josh worked until 9:30 P.M. after lunch at Harry's, stopping only once to make a run to Your Store to buy bread and sandwich meat, pop for Josh, bottled water for Katie and a giant bag of Cheetos. Even Katie uncharacteristically downed a few, then complained about her orange fingers. She was still swallowing the disappointment of not overhearing any pertinent gossip at Harry's. She was just sure she'd glean something after that editorial. She'd picked up the paper as soon as she overheard Jessica and Paul Joy talking about the editorial when she was getting in her car early that morning and they were out watering flowers. It didn't take her long to discover that Harold Crabb was one gutsy and astute guy. And he was for sure right about one thing: something was about to happen.

The next day they decided to make a run to the dump outside of town. All that hard work had produced a mound of garbage that was quite an eyesore. Katie figured Aunt Tess's neighbors had put up with enough the last few years without her creating a new reason to look away. Besides, she was also hoping things might at least begin to look marketable from the outside before contacting a local Realtor, which she hoped to do in the next couple of days. They'd already been here a week—thank goodness two of those days were teacher institute days—and Josh had to get back to school. That was that. Thank goodness at least Latin was e-mailing him assignments and he could turn in most of his papers electronically, but they had already, in a polite yet nudging e-mail to her, "certainly hoped" she'd have him back soon.

Aside from the major pieces of furniture and a few miscellaneous piles, Katie and Josh had finally nearly emptied the living room. One of the piles stacked on the gray couch was things they hoped to find the rest of, like a matching shoe or the other earring or the vacuum sweeper they speculated went with the hose. Katie would have chucked them, but Josh insisted they could bring money for Dorothy's sale, and he'd worked so hard, she gave in. There were also a couple of expensive-looking items that they had no clue about and were in hopes of perhaps finding something else that went with "it" or solved the mystery. They referred to this pile as the puzzle area.

The multiple boxes of papers caused her to moan, but she had made the decision at some point just to keep piling them up. She would go through them at her leisure when she got home. Surely the trust documents were buried somewhere among them.

After sweeping her eyes through the room, Katie decided this would be a good place to stop for the night. Tomorrow they would tackle the bedroom, which was the worst of all. The Lexus was nearly packed to the gills again, since they'd stuffed in a few extra end tables, three card tables, two footstools and a hall tree. Although Katie had been avoiding Dorothy, a run to the farm needed to be made first thing in the morning. Besides, she'd sneaked in a few phone calls, including ones to her banker, done a bit more Web browsing, studied the stock market and replayed all the possibilities. She knew it was time to make her move.

20

May Belle closed her eyes the first moment Maggie unleashed the warm stream of water on her scalp. With her husband so long-ago gone and Earl not being much of a hugger, she longed for physical touch. While Maggie chatted on about whatever, May Belle was oblivious to her words, so lost was she to the wonderful and simple sensation of warm water flowing over her head, the gentle yet thorough circular motions of Maggie's fingers as they scrubbed behind each ear and down the nape of her neck, the floral fragrance of the shampoo and then, again, the warm, flowing rinse waters. When Maggie put the towel around the back of May Belle's head and helped her sit up, she felt like she was being dragged out of a soothing cocoon.

"Don't you think?" Maggie asked.

"Don't I think what?"

"For goodness sakes, May Belle, have you heard a word I said?" Maggie patted the towel to May Belle's head, wrapped it turban style and tucked it in. She followed May Belle to the left station of the two. No need to ask; this was always the routine. Only those getting color and perms got the right chair. Since May Belle had never colored or permed her hair, let alone let anyone cut it, saying, "What's the point of paying for a cut when all I do is put it up in a knot anyway?" the routine never changed.

Maggie, of course, knew the truth about why May Belle cut her own hair; she saved costs wherever she could. Maggie sometimes wondered—and she wasn't alone in this—how May Belle and Earl managed to get by. As far as anyone knew, all the income she had was Homer's Social Security. This every-other-week routine was a necessary indulgence. Maggie had never once in all the decades she'd owned the shop upped May Belle's five-dollar ticket. Her tip always came in the form of something deliciously sweet to eat, and that was just fine with Maggie.

May Belle thunked down in the chair, and Maggie began her rhythmic pumping process to raise her to working level. Sometimes Maggie would even break out singing to the beat, although today she didn't. Maggie undid the towel and began combing through May Belle's long, white, thinning locks.

"I see you've given yourself another hatchet job." The line never changed.

"Hmmm," May Belle responded, keeping her eyes closed and her head down.

"So, what'll it be today? Spikes? Braids? Pompadour? Horse's tail?" Maggie asked as May Belle lifted her head at the end of the comb-out process. It was a ridiculous question, since May Belle always had her hair put up in a simple bun, but one Maggie always asked.

"Braids."

"*What?*"

"You heard me. Braids."

"What kind of braids?" Maggie's surprised face looked

over May Belle's shoulder as they spoke to one another in the mirror.

"The kind that look like *The Sound of Music* braids. You know, where they come up around each side of your head?"

"May Belle, are you serious?"

"Yes, I am, Maggie. It's just time for a change. I don't know another thing to say other than sometimes it's just time for a change. I used to wear my hair like that when Homer and I were courting. I've been thinking about him a lot lately, and I'm just tired of everything being the same. My hair is one thing I have control over. Of course, going back to something I wore over fifty years ago isn't exactly a change, is it?"

"Well, I'd sure say it is. It's so old it's new again! And you know how I love doing new!" Maggie parted May Belle's hair down the middle of her head. "Mind if I add a bit of a French braid touch to it?" Maggie's persona was lit up like a Christmas tree at the opportunity to do something new . . . on *anyone*! As much as she loved the hair shows and keeping her own head changing, her clientele wasn't exactly into change.

"Have at it!"

Just then the bell jingled, and Dorothy sauntered in.

"Can you believe what I just heard?" Maggie said to Dorothy.

Dorothy's heart skipped a beat. Although she hoped she could trust Katie, she had continued to feel a bit uneasy since she'd revealed her secret to anyone.

"And what would that be?" Dorothy asked hesitantly.

"May Belle here has asked for a new hairdo!"

Dorothy quick-stepped to the chair and picked up one of May Belle's wrists. "Just checking to make sure she hasn't hog-tied you in this chair, dearie. And what do you mean, a new hairdo?"

May Belle shot her head up to look at Dorothy. "It's just time for a change. Sometimes it's just time for a change."

"It must be catching," Dorothy said.

"What?" May Belle and Maggie said together.

"Change."

"Joshua Kinney. Wake up." Katie banged on his motel door at 7:15 A.M. "Get your shower. We'll have breakfast at Harry's, make a run to Dorothy's and finish our talk, then we'll get over to Aunt Tess's and begin work on the bedroom."

"Yes, ma'am." He heard his mom's departing footsteps through the door.

He tossed in bed a few times, then finally rolled out and into the bathroom. He stood under the steamy shower water, head back and eyes closed, waiting for his body to come to life. He felt achy, having moved furniture around and loading so much stuff in and out of the Lexus.

Josh knew it was peculiar that his mom wanted to eat at Harry's a second day in a row. After all, she had barely eaten a bite of her food there yesterday.

Thoughts of Dorothy and Sheba came to his mind, and he smiled. He had definitely become attached to that fun oldster and her mutt dog. Dorothy even seemed to be making a little headway into his mom's crusty hide. He was eager to be back out at the farm, if just for a little while.

Katie had to ask Josh to repeat nearly everything he said to her at Harry's. She seemed preoccupied at best and intentionally eavesdropping at worst. *Don't tell me Mom's turning into one of* them*!* He snickered to himself at the thought.

She only ate one bite of her toast, fidgeting with it, cutting it in half, spreading a wafer-thin smear of peach preserves. Doing everything but actually eating it. When Josh was just about done polishing off his "Morning Special" of two eggs, two slices of toast, hand-patted sausage patties, biscuits and gravy and a large milk, she used her cell phone to call Dorothy, even though a pay phone was right in front of her on the wall. Josh had never seen his mom use a pay phone, though she had once commented about all the germs.

"Dorothy? How are you this morning? I didn't wake you, did I? . . . Good. Josh and I were about to make a run. We're loaded up again and just wanted to make sure you were home. . . . Yes. I have thought it over and considered the details. We'll talk about it when we get there."

Squeaking stools swiveled her way. No matter how quietly she'd been talking, everyone had heard every word. *What* was *Dorothy thinking anyway, hanging around with this city slicker?* they all wondered. As far as they were concerned, she wasn't one to be trusted. No one from the city was.

Dear Lord, all I hear You saying is Trust Me. I can only assume You mean for me to trust in Katie Durbin's advice. So be it. Amen.

As usual, Dorothy was standing near the barn awaiting their arrival. Katie noticed that although Dorothy had obviously had her hair done, her face seemed drawn, as though she hadn't slept. Sheba was waiting at Josh's door before the car stopped. Katie said hello and pulled up to the giant barn doors, waiting for Josh to open them. When he did, they discovered Dorothy had dragged things around until there wasn't room to pull the Lexus in. Katie parked on the incline next to the silo and set the parking brake.

"Howdy doody, you two," Dorothy said. "I'm glad to see you this morning. Goodness me, I plumb forgot about that mess. Sorry." She walked around the car and patted Josh on the shoulder with one hand while patting Sheba's head with the other. Josh had scooped up the dog the moment he exited the car, and they were engaged in a morning hug of sorts.

Katie opened the back of the Lexus, looked inside and drew in her breath with a loud gasp.

"Joshua! Where did this come from?" She carefully pulled what looked like a large tarnished vase from between two boxes and clutched it to her chest.

"I found it behind the door in Aunt Tess's bedroom. I went to take a look in there before we left last night, trying to psych myself up for what came next. I realized something always kept the door from opening all the way. When I checked it out, there sat that vase. I think it's just full of dirt, Mom. I put it in the car before we left last night, thinking somebody might like the vase, though. Why? What's up with it?" he asked, looking at her ashen face.

She closed her eyes and ran her hand up and down the side of the urn as though stroking a soft kitty. "It's my mother's ashes."

Dorothy and Josh stood frozen, captured by the sight before them. Katie actually began to rock back and forth. When she opened her eyes, both she and Dorothy had tears streaming down their faces, such was the compassion of this older woman and the depth of Katie's moment. *Lord, heal the hurt in her heart,* Dorothy prayed to herself.

The three of them continued to stand in silence while Dorothy and Katie wiped their noses as best they could without hankies. Finally Dorothy broke into the quiet with yet another startling discovery.

"Katie, dear, perhaps this isn't the time, but somehow I feel God nudging me that it is." She walked over to the base of the silo and picked up the small square box she'd set there earlier. Katie had a quizzical look on her face until she saw the label.

"Oh, my *gosh*! Aunt Tess! I forgot all about her. Where on earth did you find *her*?"

Josh looked nothing short of dismayed.

"Well, honey, I came out here to pray yesterday, and before I went back to the house I just couldn't help but poke around a bit in some of the boxes you brought over. Imagine my surprise when I read the label on this one! I set it out here so as I wouldn't forget to give it to you. I figured it got mixed in with your boxes by accident." Both of them chuckled; Josh looked at them like they were daft, one moment crying and the next laughing. He recalled finding the box behind the driver's seat yesterday and unloading it in the barn without paying any attention.

Goosebumps raced over Katie's entire body, and her heart nearly boomed out of her chest. It struck Katie like an erupting volcano: here they were, in a manner of speaking, her mother and her mother's sister, once again reunited in front of the silo. Like the picture. Gathered with them, she and her son and the woman who had somehow brought them all together. Without a shadow of a doubt, but unable to understand or vocalize it, Katie knew this scene was meant to be. If there was a God, He had surely led her to this place, to this moment in her life.

Everything was finally unloaded but the sisters, as Josh had begun referring to them, who were now safely seat-belted into the backseat of the Lexus. Although it kind of creeped him out at first, he got used to their presence.

Finally Katie, Dorothy and Josh were gathered around Dorothy's kitchen table, each sipping water with a slice of lemon. Josh started to head up the stairs to boot up Dorothy's computer when they came inside, but Katie asked him to stay.

"Well, Katie, what have you decided? Should I accept Colton Craig's offer for the farm?"

"What?" Josh yelped. "You're thinking of selling your farm?" He looked from Dorothy to his mom, and an uneasy feeling seized him. *This is what Dorothy's been talking to Mom about? Selling her farm? This is what Mom's been up to with all her secret stuff the last couple days?* His cheeks flamed red as fear rose up within him. *So help me, Mom . . . if you've put one of your typical big-business, land-deal power plays on Dorothy and pressured her, or ripped her off in any way . . .* He could barely breathe.

"Yes. I'm afraid I have to at least think about it, dear." Dorothy's eyes shifted from Josh to Katie, then back to Josh again. "I see your mom didn't mention this to you."

"*She did not!*" He spat and emphasized each word.

Dorothy wondered what on earth had prompted such a strong response, but let it pass.

"Okay, I'm ready," Dorothy said. She sighed and methodically folded her hands in front of her. "Tell me what you think."

21

"I have an entirely new option for you to consider, Dorothy. I realize Craig & Craig's option contract expires tomorrow and you're down to the wire with decision making, but I hope it's one you'll at least consider."

Josh began drumming his fingers on the table and snorting loudly through his nose as though trying to contain himself. He glared at his mom, who he realized was wearing her close-the-deal face. He'd seen it hundreds of times throughout his life.

"I would like to buy the farm, Dorothy. I am prepared to pay you five percent more than the offer on the table."

"What on earth . . ." Dorothy's voice trailed off. Josh stood up out of his chair and looked down on his mother.

"I'm serious," Katie said. "I will pay you up front or spread it out—whatever works best for you. I have already spoken with my financial adviser and my banker, and I am in a sound position to make and carry out this offer with expedience. Of course, you wouldn't need to move until you were ready. There would be no hurry for that. No. No hurry. You could stay on as long as you like, and we'd work out a reasonable arrangement."

The three of them were silent for several seconds, Katie, posture erect, on the edge of her chair, while Josh stood and

stared bullets at his mom. Dorothy finally spoke. "I simply
do not know what to say."

"I realize this is not giving you much time for a decision,
if you'd like to consider my offer against Craig's." They all
looked from one to the other. "Joshua Matthew Kinney,
please sit down." He simply could not.

"Oh, Lordy be," Dorothy said as she shook her head
back and forth. "Lordy be and gracious me. What a mountain of mayhem this has turned out to be!"

Even in the midst of their tension, Josh and Katie shot
one another an *aha!* look. "So this is who it came from!"
Josh said.

"And what would that be?" Dorothy asked, happy for a
distraction from her thoughts and what seemed like a release of the gripping tension between mother and son.

"Mom used that phrase the other day, and when I asked
her where she'd picked that up, she couldn't remember."

"I do believe that's nearly as old as I am. No doubt you
heard your mother say it, Katie, honey. Nearly everyone
from Partonville used to say that." Dorothy studied this
mother and son across from her, and her spirit within was
suddenly stirred with a sense of hope and peace. A peace
that passes all understanding.

"Yes!" Dorothy stuck her hand out across the table to
shake on the deal.

"Are you talking about my offer?" Katie asked, her voice
rising nearly an octave.

"Yes, ma'am. I am not only talking about your offer but
also accepting it. And I am thanking God for you, His answer to my prayers. Thank you, Katie Durbin. Thank You,
Jesus." Dorothy looked up toward the heavens and hollered
out loud, "THANK YOU, JESUS!"

In astonishment at her own actions—not to mention in celebration of the easiest deal she'd ever closed—and fueled by an overwhelming and inexplicable sense of joy, Katie clasped Dorothy's hand in both of hers and began aggressively pumping it up and down. Dorothy pulled Katie to the middle of the kitchen and flung the slightly reluctant Katie into do-si-doing with her like a square dancer, causing Sheba to begin a fit of barking. Dorothy steered their way over to a stunned and worried Josh, caught him up in the action, and the three of them whirled and twirled away in the middle of the kitchen. He scowled the entire while.

Josh had no idea why Dorothy would ever have to think about selling her farm. He sure hoped his mother wasn't the one who tried to talk her into selling! Whatever, he suspected he knew what his mother's motives were for saying she wanted to buy it. *She better not have reeled Dorothy in, hook, line and sinker. Dorothy isn't one of her fat-cat clients! She's . . . DOROTHY!*

All he knew for sure was that at the moment, none of it seemed to make a bit of difference to Dorothy, who was thrilled. What would be the point of his trying to warn, argue with or question a woman who was so happily and wholeheartedly celebrating? He was helpless for the moment to do anything other than dance in her unbridled joy. But smile he would not. A shallow grin was the best he could muster.

Katie Mabel Carol Durbin, a self-proclaimed city girl, lay diagonally across the bedspread on her bed at the Lamp Post Motel in Pardon Me Ville, Illinois, fully clothed. She glanced at the clock; it was 2:30 A.M. She'd been staring at the ceiling for three hours, barely twitching a muscle. She couldn't ever remember feeling so physically and mentally tired, yet so regenerated and oddly relaxed and satisfied. To say she was blindsided by her own flurry of activities and choices was an understatement. To believe she now all but owned a farm was bizarre at best and ridiculous at worst. And yet . . . aside from the rest of the formalities, own a farm she did. The very thought—*regardless* of her motives, which even she herself wasn't sure about—made her grin. *Obviously, I've cracked up.*

Joshua Matthew Kinney sat slumped in his desk chair in front of his computer. He glanced at the clock: 2:30 A.M. He'd been trying to figure out what in the world to e-mail to Dorothy, if anything, for going on three hours. Feeling a need to warn Dorothy while intermittently composing e-mails to his mom, lashing out at her . . . her . . . Since, back in Dorothy's kitchen, his original fears about his mom's dealings with Dorothy had materialized and his fear had now turned to anger. He was so angry and worried that he couldn't even think straight.

Last night, while all that crazy dancing and document reading and talking about terms was going on, Josh had first gone upstairs and played games on Dorothy's computer, then retreated to the dark, quiet barn. He thought he might spontaneously erupt into flames. He was so angry on the way back to the Lamp Post that he couldn't even talk to his mom, not that she tried to initiate any conversation with him. They'd each gone to their rooms in silence.

Josh had tried to watch TV to distract himself, but he had way too many pent-up emotions and energies for that. He left the motel and jogged and walked and jogged again, all around Pardon Me Ville. He went down May Belle's street twice and circled the square several times, finally deciding to make his way back to the Lamp Post before he was picked up for suspicious behavior. He then booted up his computer and typed his fingers nearly to the bone, only to end up deleting every word of correspondence after correspondence. Finally, at three-fifteen he drifted off to sleep, at exactly the same time as did his mother.

Dorothy Jean Wetstra flopped down in bed at 9:15 P.M. after saying prayers of thanksgiving for thirty-five minutes. She slept like a log all night for the first time in a long while.

BANG! BANG! BANG! Josh pounded on his mother's motel door at 7:30 A.M. He hadn't brushed his teeth; he looked like a bear and acted like one, too. BANG! BANG! BANG!

Katie's voice was weak and distant-sounding through the door. "Who is it?"

"Your son."

"Josh, it's seven-thirty. Why on earth are *you* banging on *my* door?"

"We need to talk. Now."

"I agree we need to talk, but it's not going to be now. I've barely had any sleep, I'm barely awake and I'm not in the mood."

"No. I bet you aren't! Who could be after what you've done!"

"And what, exactly, have I done?"

Silence. Katie waited a moment, then repeated her question. Silence. She cracked open the door; Josh was gone. She heard the door next to hers slam shut. She'd deal with him later.

"Dear Outtamyway," he typed. He lifted his fingers from the keys, backed up his chair a bit, then realized he just couldn't bring himself to use a nickname that sounded like how his mother was treating Dorothy.

> Dear Dorothy, We have to talk. Please e-mail me as soon as you're booted up. I'll check my e-mail every five minutes. It's 7:45 a.m. We NEED to talk.
> Sincerely, Josh.

The first time he checked, she had answered.

> Josh, I was up early today and happy to find a word from you. I pray you are okay, though. You sound so distressed. Phone me.

He did so immediately, explaining that he didn't want to talk over the phone.

"Have your mom bring you out, honey."

"NO! I don't want to . . . she can't."

"All right then, me and Sheba will fire up The Tank and we'll be right there."

"I'll be waiting at the curb."

Josh hopped in the car. Before he was even settled in, The Tank lurched forward, causing his head to whip back.

"You know, Dorothy, even though I totally trust your driving," he said, working to convince himself more than anyone, "I imagine you and The Tank could scare the pants off of some people."

"Reckon we have," she said flatly. "In fact, I've nearly scared them off myself a few times, especially here lately. You're not the first to mention it. I trust God will let me know when it's time to turn in my keys, however. I just hope it's not too soon. Until then . . . !" And off they went. Where they were heading, neither of them was sure, but they were on their way.

"So what has you so troubled, Josh?"

Josh remained quiet for a few moments, and Dorothy just let him. She circled round the square twice before he spoke.

"Dorothy, I need to talk to you about what my mom's done." Dorothy turned off the square, and The Tank, like a horse heading for the barn, was heading its way to a stall at Crooked Creek.

"Oh, honey! You'll just never know how much this means to me! Your mom is an angel straight from heaven! The weight of that decision has nearly plumb worn me out lately. And then in God's perfect timing, there was Katie with her kind and generous offer."

"Timing. Mom. Offer. Right. That's what we need to talk about."

"I'll tell you, I can die in peace now. Such a blessing. I just couldn't get settled within myself about that Craig & Craig offer. Seems to me they were just after my land to make a killing."

"Killing. Land. Right. That's what I want to talk to you about. Dorothy, here's the thing. You trust my mom, right?"

"Honey, I trust God, and from the peace that washed over me when your mom made me that offer, I knew it was straight from Him."

"Dorothy, do you believe in the devil?"

She glanced at him for a moment as she rounded the corner off the highway toward the farm, then said, "Yes. Yes, I do believe there is evil in the world. But what on earth caused you to ask me that now?"

Even as angry as he was with his mom, he just couldn't seem to get out exactly what he'd been thinking. It would sound too mean. Too crazy. He somehow just knew Dorothy wouldn't want to hear that kind of comparison, since she was obviously so high on this woman whom she obviously didn't know the way he did.

"Josh, what in the world is going through your head, son?"

"Dorothy, my mom is a real hardnose when it comes to business."

"Yes, I know."

"Well, I just hope she hasn't . . ."

"Hasn't what, Josh?"

He drew in a deep breath, and his shoulders nearly

touched his earlobes before he let it out, exhaling loudly through his mouth. "Hasn't ripped you off. There. I said it."

"Did you and your mom talk on the way home last night?"

"Nope. We haven't talked since we left the farm. I tried to talk to her this morning, but she said she wasn't in the mood." Sarcasm laced his tone.

"I imagine there's a lot about this you don't know, sweetheart. Things aren't always what they appear, and your mom is a softer cookie than you might imagine."

"I don't have to imagine. I live with her, remember?"

"You know, Josh, I've watched you two since you arrived in Partonville. I don't like sticking my nose in where it doesn't belong, but I believe God and Aunt Tess have brought you two to Pardon Me Ville for a bigger reason than a funeral and house cleaning."

Josh looked at Dorothy, stunned. "Where'd you learn Pardon Me Ville?"

"Your mom told me about it last night while you were outdoors."

"She told you she called it that?"

"Yes, sir. And she told me plenty else. And I'm now convinced there's plenty she hasn't told you yet, and I'm sure not gonna steal her thunder." With that, she pulled into the Landerses' driveway and turned The Tank around, pointing back toward town. She was glad she had phoned Katie before she left this morning, just to make sure she would know where Josh had gone, intuitively suspecting, from the tone in his voice, that he hadn't informed her.

"Where are we going?" Josh asked.

"To your Aunt Tess's. That's where your mom said she'd be."

"When did you talk to my mom?"

"This morning right after I talked to you. Do you think I want to be charged with kidnapping? I mean, Sheba and I might be rascals, but we're not that dangerous!"

22

Katie sat at the kitchen table at Aunt Tess's, staring at the photo of her mom and Aunt Tess. Her eyes glanced around the table, from place mat to place mat, back to the picture again, then to the rose-colored candle, then to the little picture of her and Josh tucked in the frame. It ran through her mind that the table had begun to feel like a shrine. A place of order in the midst of chaos. She couldn't help but wonder if Aunt Tess, in her own crazy way, had clung to her last remnants of sanity at this table. Waiting. But for whom and what?

She retrieved a rectangular box of kitchen matches from atop the stove and stood over the table. A sense of reverence overtook her as she struck the wooden match, quickening to the sound of the strike, smelling the essence of the puff of smoke, drinking in the sight of the flame as it flared, then settled into a slow burn. She briefly pondered how pleasurable was the simple striking of an old-fashioned kitchen match. She set the box down, picked up the candle and for the first time smelled its wax. Roses! It smelled of roses—her favorite. She put the candle back down in the saucer, straightened the wick and ignited it. Staring unblinking into the small flame, she seated herself before it, moving the photographs into its light.

Unaware of the sound of her own voice, she began

humming "Amazing Grace," the song her mother used to sing to her when she was little. The song her mother sang out loud all the days of her life.

She stared at the face of her mother, candlelight now illuminating her familiar features. Katie closed her eyes and tried to imagine what her mother would look like today, more than ten years older than when last she saw her, last heard her sing. Straining to remember the exact sound of her mother's voice, she suddenly realized *she* was singing aloud. Her throat clutched, and yet she could not stop singing the words to which she had previously paid no attention.

"Amazing grace . . ."—tears welling in her eyes—"how sweet the sound"—overflowing her lashes—"that saved a wretch like me . . ." A sob surged up from deep within her belly and interrupted the words. Even so, she didn't stop singing. "I once was lost, but now I'm found, was blind but now I see." She sniffled a bit, then very softly began speaking.

"Could it be, God, that You would use me to answer someone else's prayer? Could it be? Could it be that You *do* listen? Is it possible that I have heard YOU?"

Katie heard the front door fling open. Quickly she wiped her eyes and composed herself. Although she started to blow the candle out, she changed her mind, the fragrance of rose now filling the kitchen. She stood up just as Josh entered, Dorothy close behind.

Joshua and Katie stood staring at one another, trying to read each other's face. Katie looked at Dorothy, who nodded her head, then silently walked on through the kitchen—Josh watched, a pleading look in his eyes, but she just swept right past him, Sheba at her heels—and went out the back door into the yard, where she parked herself on the porch and began to pray.

"Sit down, Joshua. We need to talk." Katie's voice was firm yet pensive. Josh pulled out a chair, seating himself back a ways from the table, as though pulling in too close might send a wrong message.

"Joshua Matthew Kinney, I know you're angry at me." He looked away from her face and stared at the candle. "You are the one who first told Dorothy I was in real estate, remember?

"Hmph." His eyes blinked slowly and his head nodded, affirming her statement. Still he didn't look at her.

"Dorothy asked me for advice. Dorothy asked me," she said, emphasizing each word.

Josh's head snapped in her direction. "Oh, and wasn't *that* handy? She asked you. You, who care more about the color of money and landing a deal than just about *anything*—including me!" He had never so brazenly spoken his emotions like this, and right to his mother's face! Years of wounds suddenly rose up out of a buried place, the bite of his words surprising even him. It was Katie's turn to break eye contact, once again looking at the flame, her own son's hateful glare piercing her heart.

She took a deep breath, held it for a moment, then sighed, willing herself to look back into his eyes. What she discovered was the raw and revealing face of a little boy. Her child. Her son. Her baby. After having so abruptly spoken the hurt of his soul, Josh was left emotionally naked. Tears sprang into Katie's eyes. She reached her right hand forward to touch Josh's cheek. Out of reflex, he snapped his head back, blinking back his own tears.

Katie withdrew her hand, gripping it in her left, then

wringing them together. She recognized a bare longing and neediness in her son—which reflected *her* innermost self, her innermost self that had for so many years been crusted over.

"Oh, Joshua. Deals aren't the only thing I care about." Like strangers circling one another, deciding on issues of trust before moving too close, their eyes searched and darted, trying to penetrate the exterior.

"You, Joshua, you are the best deal I have ever made." Never had he heard such conviction in his mother's voice. Such tenderness. He slumped forward in his chair, elbows on his knees, fingers entwined, head hanging down so she couldn't see his eyes.

Katie rose out of her chair and knelt down in front of him, cupping her hands over his—not unlike the way Pastor had done with hers one short week ago. "You, Joshua, are the best gift I've ever been given." With her right index finger, she tilted his chin so he was looking at her, then leaned in very close and kissed his cheek. They were both full-out weeping now. Tentatively, waiting for the acceptance of her gestures, she put her hands on his shoulders. Then, still on her knees, she pressed her cheek against his and hugged him.

For a moment, he didn't respond—but he didn't reject her either. Before too long, one hand moved to her back, then the other. The embrace lasted for several moments.

While the fragrance of roses filled their senses and the light of a single candle softened their surroundings, Dorothy, still out on the back porch, just kept on a-prayin' until her spirit sensed it was time to quit.

When Dorothy entered the kitchen, she found Katie and Josh taping up a couple of boxes. She searched one face, then the next. When they both broke out in a smile, she knew God Almighty had once again "done His thing!" There was no need for her to speak a word, other than to whisper an "Amen."

The three of them simultaneously seated themselves at the table. The table that, it suddenly seemed, so long ago had been prepared for their arrival.

23

The conversation around the kitchen table went on an hour and a half before any of them was willing to push their chairs back and get on with life. So rooted in the moment were they that they even skipped going to breakfast. Between the three of them, they ate everything in the house—a giant bag of potato chips, the rest of the Cheetos, three candy bars and a half-gallon of orange juice. Katie said she just couldn't do "that" to her body, but she did—though, truth be told, Dorothy and Josh did most of the consuming.

Katie knew she and Josh still had a long way to go to get their relationship on a healthier track, but they were headed in the right direction, she was sure of it. And if Dorothy Jean Wetstra had anything to say about it, they would stay aimed thataway until they arrived.

Katie just listened, rather than defending herself, while Dorothy explained to Josh the evolution of the sale, how it was his *mom* who had come up with the idea of making sure there would always be a place to hunt for crawdads.

"Crooked Creek Park. Now, how does *that* suit ya?" she asked him, beaming from ear to ear herself at the very idea of it. "Why, she's even gonna help me go through the procedure with the conservation department *before* I draw up the papers with *her,* just so that land can be donated by my family, in my family's name." Dorothy placed her hand over her heart, closed her eyes and spoke a quiet "Thank You, Jesus."

Katie pursed her lips, feeling slightly guilty. Yes, that was the deal. But she also knew any land developed around a park would definitely bring a much higher price tag. Nevertheless, much to her surprise, she had been moved to give Dorothy—and every family member in her photo albums, ancient and new—that privilege and tax break, rather than closing the deal and taking the tax cut herself. She recognized her own generosity as nothing short of a miracle. Yes, perhaps there really *was* a God!

It was as though a veil had been lifted from Katie's eyes, about a lot of things. For the first time in a long time, as she studied Joshua, she saw, really saw, the essence of her son—apart from the shadow of his father. Josh caught her staring at him several times throughout the morning, and finally asked her to stop it.

"Well, anyone who's as handsome a devil as you are, Joshmeister, deserves a good gander," Dorothy said. Although he found it all a bit embarrassing, he obviously relished the attention from both these women.

"Where are you going to go, Dorothy, once you're ready to move out?" Josh asked. "And how long do you think it'll take before you're *ready* to move out?"

"Me oh my!" she exclaimed. "I haven't a clue, but I bet The Big Guy does!"

"Big guy?" Josh asked.

"Yup. The Big Guy who brought me your mother," she said, pointing heavenward. He looked at his mom, expecting her to protest. Instead, she just shrugged her shoulders and grinned.

As dew settles on the grass, it simultaneously came over

all of them that it was time to get to work. Dorothy jumped up and said she'd shake the crumbs out of the place mats while they loaded up the boxes. "These place mats are just like the ones at my house!" she exclaimed. "This is the first I noticed that!"

Katie nearly choked on the last of her orange juice. "Of COURSE!" she hollered, causing them to jump. "Why didn't I think of that before! It's so obvious!"

"Gosh, Mom. Settle down. What's so obvious?"

"Dorothy! Why don't you buy *this* place? I mean, it's in town, close to your friends, not too big. And it's soon to be available!"

Dorothy first just kind of reared her head back, then blinked a few times, appearing to Katie as though she was trying to clear her vision so her brain might jump-start.

"Of course, I'd have it good and sanitized for you. Take care of that buckling cement out front . . ."

"Well," Dorothy said hesitantly, running her finger up and down the familiar ruffle on the place mat. "Well . . . I guess I could at least entertain the notion." She stood up, cocked her hip and placed her left hand on her hip and her right hand to her cheek. She stayed in place but slowly turned in a semicircle, pursing her lips, nodding her head, occasionally shrugging her shoulders.

"We'll work a trade for a portion of the farm," Katie said. Josh warily eyed his mother, raising an eyebrow at her when she looked toward him.

"Let's take a look at the rest of the place, Sheba," Dorothy said. "See how it *feels*." Sheba jumped to attention the minute Dorothy stood, ready to move with her master.

Dorothy and Sheba walked from room to room, Katie and Josh staying their distance, but within eye range. Dorothy stood in the center of the living room, looking from window to door to back wall, trying to picture herself here . . . what her life might be like in a place this size. Actually, trying to picture herself and what her life might be like *anywhere* that wasn't the farm. It was the first time she'd truly felt the reality of her decisions. *I am going to leave the farm!* Even though she felt a bit queasy at the thought, she would never forget the absolute peace that washed through her when, out at the farm, she'd accepted Katie's deal. Yes, whenever she doubted her decision, that's what she went back to: that peace that passes all understanding, and it only came from one place.

Silently, and with her imagination fully awake, she step-by-methodical-step moved into the hall, then into the bathroom and on to the bedroom, praying her way through the entire place.

Katie noticed Dorothy staring into dirty corners and at hazy windows, up at cobwebbed ceilings and cracked tiles on the bathroom floor. Josh cleared his throat rather loudly, but didn't speak.

"Of course, I'd get the place in tip-top condition, up to building codes and all for you," Katie said, maintaining her enthusiastic tone. "I'd eat the cost of the upgrades, throw in new carpeting in the living room, if you'd like, and . . . make sure you had appropriate telephone lines for your computer! Josh and I discovered, one day when we tried to boot up from here, that Aunt Tess still had her old rotary phone lines wired right into the wall. Yes, I'd make sure issues like that are covered."

Dorothy just stared at her, first expressionless, then squinting a bit, as though sizing her up.

Eventually, like a tiny parade, the three worked their way

back into the kitchen, stopping in front of the sink. They all watched Sheba run back under the kitchen table, where she'd been before all the action, wind herself back in a little ball by the heat register—even though it wasn't turned on—sigh and instantly close her eyes to snooze.

Dorothy began to laugh, then said, "That settles it! Sheba just made us a deal!" She extended her hand toward Katie at the same time she glanced at Josh—who was scowling. Just before Katie took hold of her hand, Dorothy swiftly withdrew hers, leaving Katie reaching for air.

"And don't think I won't hold you to *all* that, missy, especially that fair-trade part for a portion of my current estate." She winked at Josh. "Why, I recall hearing somebody—who is supposedly quite the real estate wheeler-dealer—say she thought this place ought to be bulldozed into a hole!"

First Katie burst out laughing, then all of them did.

"Dorothy, you have a steel-trap mind, for sure! And I'm beginning to think you and Josh could be dangerous if you spent too much time together!"

Before Dorothy left Aunt Tess's, she stood in the living room doorway and once again scanned the living room. Actually, the thought of decorating her own place—for the very first time in her life, since she'd simply carried on her life where she'd been raised—kind of excited her!

"May Belle!" Dorothy exclaimed when May Belle opened the door. "You'll just never guess what all has happened!"

"Well, come in and close the door, dear, unless you want to keep standing on the front porch doing all that yelling." Dorothy and May Belle made their way to the kitchen.

Sheba was already standing in the middle of the floor waiting for a goodie when they arrived. May Belle went to the refrigerator, rummaged around until she produced a slice of cheese, then began feeding it to Sheba in pieces.

"Honestly, May Belle! Aren't you the least bit curious about my news?"

"Of *course* I am! I figured you'd spill the beans when you were good and ready."

"I've sold the farm!"

May Belle snapped her head in Dorothy's direction, accidentally holding the piece of cheese midair rather than tossing it. Finding it just out of her reach, Sheba began jumping up and down, yapping. May Belle tossed her the chunk without looking her way. A stunned look was plastered on her face, and her mouth was wide open.

"I don't think I heard you correctly."

"Yup. You did."

"You sold the farm? You sold Crooked Creek Farm? To whom?" May Belle thunked down in the chair, her knees feeling a bit weak.

"Katie Durbin."

"You sold the farm to Katie Durbin?"

"Yup." They sat there in silence for a moment while May Belle digested what she was hearing.

"When are you going to move? Where are you going to go? When did all this happen?"

"I sold the farm yesterday. I'll move when I'm plumb good and ready and have figured out what to do with a lifetime full of stuff. And I'm going to be moving right around the corner from you and Earl into Tess's old place, which I just purchased within the hour. Well, traded a slice of farm for. After all these years, we'll be NEIGHBORS! Won't that just be the berries?"

May Belle nodded her head. "Of course. If you say so, dear." She suddenly felt as if she were living in a fog.

"Well, I say so, but I've even got *more* to say. What do you think about that?"

"I'm not sure my poor old heart can take anymore."

"I've saved the best for last." For the next half-hour, Dorothy shared the utter joy in her heart about Crooked Creek Park. She talked about how she could picture people picnicking there and younguns running free and splashing in the creek . . . it would be a part of nature until the Good Lord decided otherwise.

Once May Belle got over the shock, she couldn't help but be relieved that her best friend in the whole world would, before long, be safely sleeping just a few doors away. For this, she was very happy, even though she knew Dorothy had a long road ahead of her.

"I've just got one worry about all of this, my Dearest Dorothy," she finally said.

"What's that?"

"That nary a cookie or cake will ever be safe on my countertop again!"

Once Katie knew the immediate pressure to sell Aunt Tess's house was removed, she didn't feel the same need to press on to finish up the house-clearing task. Although they were pretty close, there was still at least another couple days' work left on that part alone—not to mention the sanitizing and everything else she'd promised—and it was Thursday already. Like a last-hour reprieve, it came to her that they could now just lock the place up and leave it until summer break. Get both of them back into their own beds for a couple of nights before Josh headed back to school on Monday. Dorothy had already said she couldn't even think about moving until after the auction, which probably wouldn't take place until at least midsummer anyway. "And believe you me, there will be a whopper of an auction for *this* downsize!"

It was 7:00 P.M. when Josh and Katie had finished packing up the Lexus. They were on their way to Dorothy's with their last run for the day when Katie made the announcement. "Joshua, I've decided we're going to head back to Chicago tomorrow. I hope we can get on the road by nine or so and beat Friday-night rush-hour traffic around the city." She glanced at Josh, who immediately began what she predicted might come.

"Mom! We've still got lots to do, and you promised Dorothy . . ."

"Josh. I will keep *all* my promises, including promising you right now that I will keep all my promises!" She spoke in a stern tone, desiring to make known her honest intentions and keep another storm at bay. "The fact is, sooner or later, we *have* to get home, and you need to get back to school. We can come back and finish up in June when school's out. Take our time. Dorothy already told us she wasn't going to be moving until maybe even late summer. Besides, that'll give us something to look forward to."

"*You* look forward to coming back?"

Katie slowed down the moment gravel began spitting up

on the undercarriage. They drove along for a bit, just listening to the clatter-bang.

"The honest truth?" Katie asked.

"Yes."

"Yes. I must admit, I'll look forward to coming back for a visit. And I must admit that no one is more surprised about that fact than I."

Dorothy, Josh and Katie sat in the kitchen at the farm eating breakfast at 8:00 on Friday morning. The Lexus was now packed with their belongings and several boxes of paperwork, readied for the sifting. Dorothy had absolutely insisted they not leave town without Josh's having a full belly. Besides, as she'd told them the night before, "I want to give you a proper Pardon Me Ville salute on your way out." She cooked them up a huge country breakfast of scrambled eggs, bacon, fried potatoes and toast. Katie watched Josh mimic Dorothy, pouring sugar all over his lavishly buttered toast, and sighed. "Not only could you two be dangerous together, but I'm beginning to think you're two peas in a pod already!"

"Yes," said Dorothy, "I imagine Joshmeister and Outtamyway could cause a mountain of mayhem without even trying!" They all laughed and laughed, until finally their chuckling died down into silence when they realized they were done eating . . . and it was time to go.

Katie looked at her watch. Josh sighed. Dorothy sprang up from the table, announcing that they all had to do what needed to be done.

"Mom, are you sure I have to . . ."

"Yes, son." She'd never called him that before. The word

son hung in the air like Tinkerbell, flittering light and pixie dust between them.

"It's sure too bad you couldn't have stayed for the Wild Musketeers game tomorrow. *That* would surely give you something to talk about to those city folks! In fact, it should keep you entertained all weekend just imagining me wielding pom-poms!"

"I must admit, Dorothy, I am curious about that," Katie said.

"I'm more curious about your catcher," Josh said. He grinned at Dorothy.

By this time, they'd walked to the Lexus, and now they stood awkwardly looking at one another. Finally Dorothy sprang forward and threw her arms around Josh. "You better send me an e-mail the minute you two get home, Joshmeister. Don't keep me awake all night wondering if you made it."

"Yes, ma'am. I promise to send you one every day. I'll give Alex your e-mail address, too. He likes meeting new people. Maybe he can come back with us this summer and join our next hunting expedition?" He looked toward his mom, who said she didn't imagine there'd be any trouble with that. Katie also assured Dorothy she would draw up rough-draft documents for her review before completing the final version, and get them in the mail in the next couple of weeks.

Katie steadied herself, knowing that undoubtedly Dorothy was going to grab her next—which she did. "Now, you two take care of each other, hear?"

"Yes, ma'am." Katie patted Dorothy on the back. Dorothy just held tight.

Josh scooped Sheba up and hugged her. "You take care

of Dorothy, okay?" She licked his cheek several times before he set her down.

"Oh, and wait a second, Dorothy." Katie opened the back door of the Lexus. "I've got something for *you* to take care of while we're gone." Her head disappeared into the backseat area while she fumbled around for a few moments. She backed out with a box in one hand and a vase in the other—the ashes of her family.

"Since Mom and my Aunt Tess loved this place so much, and since the photo of them together in front of this silo obviously meant something to both of them, I'd like to leave their remains together here in the barn for now, if you don't mind."

Dorothy gave Katie her okay by tenderly smiling and nodding her head, then reaching out and touching Katie's left cheek with the palm of her hand.

Katie walked across the barn to Dorothy's favored spot, then set the containers next to the door. "There now, ladies, you can once again enjoy the view together."

In silence Josh and Katie got into the SUV and buckled themselves in. Katie turned over the engine. "Bye! Goodbye! *Adios! Ciao!* Bye!" Josh hollered out the window as they took off down the lane.

Katie waved over her shoulder, looking in the rearview mirror—seeing a blur of pink, waving and waving and waving back. . . .

24

Back in Chicago, Katie was struck anew by how horrid traffic was, how noisy life suddenly seemed. Although she didn't dare mention it to Joshua, the thought flew through her head that this just might be their last summer in the city. Katie Mabel Carol Durbin might actually end up to be just a little more country girl than she'd ever imagined.

Dorothy waited until she knew everyone would be settled into Harry's for breakfast before she began her drive into town. It was Saturday morning; the place would be packed. She'd determined one thing: they might as well hear the news straight from her before Cora Davis got wind of it.

As she drove down her lane toward the gravel road, she wondered how it would feel when she made this journey for the last time as a resident of Crooked Creek Farm. Acutely aware of the powerful presence the land held in her life, she also knew she couldn't go anywhere God wasn't, and that knowledge is what would sustain her—as it always had.

Her mind moved from one thought to the next as she drove slowly along, passing by the Landerses' place, wondering how they'd take the news. How their lives might or might not change. How she'd sleep in a new bedroom, only the second bedroom she'd call her own in her entire life. And yet . . . she found herself just itchin' to breathe new life back into Tess's place, maybe even paint that kitchen ceiling fire engine red! Where *that* notion had come from, she had no earthly idea. But wouldn't *that* get townsfolk to talkin'? *As though they're not going to have plenty to jaw on when I get through at Harry's this morning!*

She gazed upon the fields, knowing she'd have to make at least once-weekly trips, Lord willing, to Crooked Creek Park once it was established. No way could she survive too long without planting her feet firmly in the soil. "Crooked Creek Park," she said aloud to Sheba. She just couldn't get her fill of the idea. Made her beam every time.

Looking "down the road," as her dad used to say whenever it was time for a change, she saw the bend a quarter mile ahead and gunned it. "No sense slowing down now, huh, Sheba!" Gravel spit from behind her wheels as The Tank kicked into high gear.

"Are we there yet?" she hollered over her shoulder. Sheba, head out the window, tilted her nose to the sky, sniffed once and honest-to-goodness shook her head up and down.

Cora Davis stood up like a bolt. Her natural instincts caused her body to flip into "Full Alert Ready-to-Repeat!" mode. Dorothy Jean Wetstra had, without ceremony, stood up from her stool, asked for everyone's attention and said, in her best band-director's voice, "Listen carefully, I only want to say all this one time.

"You can put the rumors to rest. *I* have sold my farm. I have sold my farm to Katie Durbin. A portion of the land will become Crooked Creek Park, for now and forever." She paused for just a hitch, but decided to continue right on before anyone could speak. "There will be a big auction this summer. I will be moving into Tess Walker's house and most likely paint the kitchen ceiling red. Amen." *I just couldn't help myself.*

Cora Davis, like everyone else, was having trouble stringing all that together—especially since Dorothy had ended her talk with the red ceiling part and now sat down and began sipping her coffee as though nothing had happened.

A blanket of silence covered everyone. Arthur looked to Gladys, who looked to Harold, who looked to Lester, who . . . Brows were furrowed around the room as they searched to untangle this startling announcement. All eyes finally turned to Dorothy, who was happily gobbling down her sweet roll like there was no tomorrow.

As though the bell had rung on Wall Street, they all started talking at once. To one another. To Dorothy. To nobody in particular.

"Well, I'll be," Arthur said. "I'll be." Sitting next to Dorothy, he reached over and patted her on the back so hard she thought for a moment she'd been slugged. "Congratulations, Dorothy! At least somebody's got more guts than jawbone around here." He looked directly at Gladys when he spoke. Whether it was intentional or not, Gladys wasn't sure.

"*What* is Katie Durbin going to do with the place?" Gladys asked in an accusatory tone.

"I have no earthly idea," Dorothy said, speaking truth—although she had her suspicions.

"You mean to tell me you sold that land to someone who might turn it into a . . . a . . ."

"Gladys, cool your jets." She'd heard Josh use that expression, and it so tickled her she was glad to have an occasion to pass it on. Gladys huffed and bristled, tossed her money on the counter and stormed herself right out the door. She had things to look into . . . although she was already picturing herself presiding at the ribbon-cutting ceremony for Crooked Creek Park!

Arthur, having had time to digest things a bit more, said, "The only thing I'll worry about is that Miss Durbin will park that traitor Lexus where I have to look at it. Can you write something in your contract about THAT?"

Dorothy laughed. It felt very good to know that Arthur, as cantankerous as he could be, was standing beside her . . . even though he probably wasn't kidding about not wanting to look at the Lexus. "Not only that, Arthur, but I'll make sure The Tank stops by for regular visits, just so you don't get too lonesome and rusty yourself."

Harold Crabb walked up behind Dorothy and put his hands on her shoulders. "I knew it! I just *knew* it! I knew something was brewing with you. I'm happy to know my reporter's nose hasn't died. I sure don't have to wonder what story I'll be running the next few editions!"

The page one headline of Sunday's edition of the *Partonville Press* unfortunately qualified poor Harold for his next misleading headline award: "Durbin Buys the Farm."

Dorothy had granted Harold an official interview immediately following the commotion at Harry's. He reported it just as Dorothy said it: "We intend for Crooked Creek Park to be a minimum of twenty acres, including the swimmin' hole, Weeping Willy, Woodsy and Willoway. Crooked

Creek Park will be a place for picnickers and visitors, town folks and tourists, to find respite for their weary souls, drink of the land's healing powers and catch a crawdad or two.

"As for me, well, I figure I'll continue to be friends with the Happy Hookers, eat at Harry's, get my hair done by Maggie, play first clarinet and eat dessert first—same as I've always done."

A Note from the Author

I am happy to have this chance to share, since I, too, am always curious about authors. Here's what I've learned from this side of the pen: writers are no more fascinating than any reader I've ever met. The only difference is, writers never seem to run out of words!

I didn't begin writing until I was in my forties (talk about a backlog of words), and I haven't stopped writing since. Our two sons are grown and gone; my husband, George, faithfully cheers me on, and leaves me alone when necessary. I once left him a note on the kitchen table that said, "I'm not here, not even when you see me." Yes, he's used to me by now.

I love what I do, which is to write (and speak) about life. One thing that never changes is the power of story. I believe God speaks to us through stories—ours, others', fiction; good, bad, dubious—and that each moment of each day delivers the potential for us to listen, learn and grow through them. As with my fictional characters, in real life, we don't always get it right, but God is always there to shine a light on a better path while loving us all the while.

'Tis that sovereign presence and graciousness of God, Dear Readers, that keeps me writing.

–Charlene Ann Baumbich
www.welcometopartonville.com

Welcome to Partonville,

home to some of the most endearing folks you've ever met—especially retired former bandleader eighty-seven-year-old Dorothy Wetstra. If she's gunning her 1976 Lincoln, trying to catch crawdaddies, whipping up an impromptu dinner-party menu of leftovers, talking to the Big Guy, making a wisecrack or giving a big hug to someone who needs one, she lives life flat-out. Dorothy is facing some big changes in her life, but shaking things up is what she does best, so pull up a chair and get ready for fireworks, laughter and we'll-get-through-it-all-with-faith friendships.

Dearest Dorothy, Are We There Yet?
ISBN 0-14-200379-4 $10.95

Dearest Dorothy, Slow Down, You're Wearing Us Out!
ISBN 0-14-200418-9 $10.95

And look for the third *Dearest Dorothy* novel soon.

For more information, visit
www.welcometopartonville.com

Available from Penguin